The Norths Sail into a Briny and Deadly Deep—On a
VOYAGE INTO VIOLENCE

"Like Conan Doyle's London, the Lockridges' New York has a lasting magic. There are taxis waiting at every corner, special little French restaurants, and perfect martinis. Even murder sparkles with big city sophistication. For everyone who remembers New York in the Forties and for everyone who wishes he did."

—Emma Lathen

"The versatility of Frances and Richard Lockridge knows almost no bounds."

—*New York Times*

"This husband and wife team is unexcelled in the field of mystery writing when it comes to a completely entertaining crime story."

—*St. Louis Post-Dispatch*

Pam and Jerry North made their first appearance in *The New Yorker* in the 1930s. In 1940, Richard Lockridge's first book-length mystery, *The Norths Meet Murder,* was published. Richard and Frances Lockridge went on to write dozens of Mr. and Mrs. North books, as well as numerous other mysteries. The Norths became the stars of a Broadway play and a movie as well as a long-running radio program and popular television series.

Books by Richard and Frances Lockridge

Death Takes a Bow
The Judge Is Reversed
Murder by the Book
Murder Comes First
Murder in a Hurry
Murder Is Served
Murder Within Murder
Voyage Into Violence

Published by POCKET BOOKS

1

Pamela North stepped out into the passage-way and encountered a man wearing a sword. The sword was long, and its hilt was gold-encrusted. The man wore, also, a red tunic, belted and criss-crossed with white webbing, and blue trousers, striped with the red of the tunic. He wore a peaked white cap, banded in red. This was not at all what Pamela North had expected to see; she had rather hoped to see Jerry. Pam withdrew into the stateroom and closed the door slowly, but very firmly.

"What," Pam North said, speaking aloud to the cabin's emptiness, "what kind of ship is this, anyway? Where the officers wear swords? What have we got ourselves into?"

She waited briefly for an answer, and received none. She went carefully to the door and, carefully, opened it again. The man with the sword was receding along the corridor. He appeared to be walking with purpose, and he was, clearly, looking straight ahead. There was no doubt that he was wearing a sword; no doubt of the red tunic. Pam averted her eyes, looked in the other direction along the corridor. Jerry North approached, not wearing a sword. Pam went several steps to meet him.

"We," she said, "have been boarded. Men with swords. They're all over the place. Pirates? Before we even leave the pier? Or is he the captain?"

Jerry North looked at his wife, an activity in which he usually found pleasure. He looked at her, now, with uneasiness, and ran a hand through his hair. He spoke very slowly, forming each word clearly.

"Are you," Jerry said, "all right?"

"I saw a man with a sword," Pam North said, with equal clarity. "Right here. A minute ago. A sword, and a uniform all colors and if captains wear swords, I'm not going." She paused. "Binoculars," she said. "Not swords."

"Oh," Jerry said, "an Old Respectable. What we've been waiting for."

"Not I," Pam said. She looked at Jerry with doubt. "Does what you just said mean something? If you're saying I'm old. And respectable isn't anything to make a point of."

They would, Jerry said, go where it was quiet. They would sit down. They would have cigarettes. He put an arm around Pam's shoulders and led her back to the stateroom. He closed the door. He lighted her a cigarette. He said it was very simple, although perhaps a little unexpected. He said they were, indeed, all over the ship. The Coral Café, where he had gone to see about a table, was full of them.

"With swords?" Pam said.

Not commonly with swords, Jerry North admitted. But with uniforms of all colors, as she said. They had come aboard with rifles. "Because," he said, "they are the Ancient and Respectable Riflemen. On their annual encampment.''

"On a ship?'' Pam said. "This ship? Why?''

"Yes,'' Jerry said. "Yes. I don't know. Probably, it's like a convention. A get-together. Last year they had it at a hotel in the White Mountains. But that was in late July.'' He paused. "I stood in line between two of them,'' Jerry said. "They explained themselves.''

"They might well,'' Pam said. "A—a kind of Boy Scout troop? They're old for it. The man with a sword—late-ish fifties, if a year. And lower two hundreds, if you come to that. And, you haven't explained the sword.''

He could not, Jerry said. Those in the café, arranging as he had been arranging for assigned seats in the dining saloon, had been innocent of swords. But he could guess—the sword was a symbol of authority. Presumably, therefore, the wearer was on a tour of duty, set apart from his duty-free fellows. It could, therefore, be assumed that he was on watch.

"Probably,'' Jerry said, "as Respected Officer of the Day. The chap who heads them up is a Respected Captain. Respected Captain Folsom. There are ten more coming. Their bus went to a wrong pier. Wrong river, actually. They're the ones we're waiting for now.'' He paused. "I was in line quite a while,'' he added, in explanation.

He had made good use of his time, Pam admitted. Bill Weigand could not have done better. Which brought up the point—where were the Weigands? She was told that they would be along, that—

There was a knock on the door of stateroom 93, A Deck, S.S. *Carib Queen,* cruise ship about to sail—as soon as ten Ancient and Respectable Riflemen found their way to her—on an eight-day voyage to Havana and Nassau. Jerry opened the door. Dorian and Bill Weigand said they were reporting in. Dorian said that there seemed to be a good many soldiers aboard. "Or something," she added.

"One of them has a sword," Pam said. "They're riflemen. Jerry's got us seated. Anyway—" Jerry nodded. "And," Pam said, "we've got a bottle somewhere in a bucket, because we have to get outside before the bars open. Outside the limit, I mean."

Bill said they knew what she meant, and that they would be right back. They went into their own cabin, next that of the Norths'. They were right back, and a steward brought, from "somewhere," a bottle of champagne in a bucket of ice. They toasted their own brief freedom, at a little after noon of a Friday in early October—freedom from an office and from authors, from an apartment and cats, from a sketch pad (although that freedom was unlikely to be exercised), from the indefensible crime of murder.

Pam was, to be sure, uneasy—when she thought of it—over her freedom from cats. But Martha had promised, and Martha was reliable. Daily she would feed the cats; she would even, from time to time, converse with them, explaining that it would be only a few days, really, before all would be as it had always been. The cats would be impatient—since for cats all change is bad, and the absence of selected humans the worst of all—but they would survive. On the next day week they would be profane in greeting, but they would forgive.

"Table for four," Jerry was telling Bill, while Pam thought briefly of her cats. "Near the captain's table. Quite choice, from the diagram. You must know a man who knows a man. Norths and Weigands, I said, and they said, 'Oh. Captain *Weigand?*' Fame? Or influence?"

There was a man he had run into once, Captain Weigand admitted. He admitted it almost drowsily. He had mentioned to the man that he and his wife, and a Mr. and Mrs. North, were cruising on the *Carib Queen*. Bill looked tired, Jerry thought; very often he looked tired. "Right," Bill said, as if Jerry had spoken, "the first two days, I sleep. If somebody sticks somebody with this sword of Pam's, don't wake me up."

"Bill!" Pam said. "It's a toy sword. And they're Boy Scouts, really. Only older and, of course, fatter. Jerry found out all about them. They're camping out."

"Meanwhile," Dorian Weigand said, "we're moving. Should we go and watch the skyline pass?"

For answer, Jerry held up the champagne bottle. It was still half full.

"I only asked," Dorian said, and swung one slim leg so that she sat on her foot. "I'll be as blasé as anyone. Try me."

Jerry filled her glass.

A loud-speaker, with a British accent, announced the first luncheon sitting.

"We're second-sitting types," Pam said, and looked at Jerry and said, "I hope?" Jerry nodded.

They sipped champagne, while the *Carib Queen* pulsated gently under them. They finished the champagne. It was Pam who suggested that, while they waited, they might go "topside" and see the ship. She was looked at. "I mean upstairs," Pam said. "Or do we go up a ladder?" She was looked at again, and admitted she had been reading up. She had, Jerry told her gently, been reading the wrong things. She had not, as she seemed to think, joined the Navy. But, nevertheless, they went.

They got lost at first, which is inevitable at first. But they found a staircase leading up, and went up it; they found the promenade deck and walked around it, and the *Carib Queen* progressed tenderly through the Narrows. She was a small and bright and perky ship, done in green and white, and everywhere she shone. Aft, on the promenade deck, was the swimming pool, empty of water and with a netting over it of heavy rope. There were also deck chairs, standing in good order. They paused to rent chairs from a deck steward in a white jacket. Already, there was no hurry about anything, and the sun was shining brightly.

They had left the deck, and were in a wide corridor separating the forward lounge from the smoking lounge—there were, Pam noted, going to be plenty of spaces to sit down—when the public-address system cleared its metallic throat and announced the second luncheon sitting. They went aft again, and down, and sat at a table for four near the center of a big room—and near two large round tables, which were in the center of the room. One of them, forward of the other, was presided over by a handsome youngish man with the four stripes of a captain on his sleeves. The table aft appeared to be presided over by a gray-haired man, with a red face. He was compressed into a red tunic. "Respected Captain Folsom," Jerry told them, and Folsom looked at them—his hearing seemed acute— and beamed pleasantly. Jerry nodded and the others smiled with the detached politeness of the unintroduced.

"Does he," Pam asked, in a much lower voice, "get to captain a table? Like the real captain?" She indicated, with a just perceptible motion of her head, the "real" captain at the other big table. Jerry doubted it; Bill Weigand shook his head, underscoring doubt.

A white-jacketed steward hovered, advised in agreeable cockney. Already, New York seemed distant, although Brooklyn still progressed slowly past them to port. (Or they could presume it did; the dining saloon was windowless.)

"Is that—" Pam asked, indicating the officer with four stripes.

"Staff captain, ma'am," the steward told her. "Captain Smythe-Hornsby, ma'am. A bit of the fish, ma'am?" Pam had a bit of the fish. The others had bits of the fish. "Ship's captain's on the bridge, ma'am," the steward said. "Some of the sprouts, ma'am?" Pam had some of the sprouts. Jerry turned away in horror; Dorian shook her head; Bill had some of the sprouts. "Trifle looks nice today," the steward said.

A tall man, notable for grooming, for the neat fit of a sports jacket, stood by the table over which Respected Captain Folsom presided. The tall man was an assured man, late on in his fifties, with a heavily handsome face. "Sit anywhere, I guess," Captain Folsom told him, in the accents of New England. "Skipper's on duty, they tell me."

The tall man said, "Thank you," and sat.

"Well, well," Bill Weigand said. "Well, well, well. J. Orville in the flesh." He spoke in a low voice, but now, as the room filled, conversation rose in it, so that there was little danger of being overheard.

They looked at Bill and waited.

"J. Orville Marsh," Bill said. "The well-known private—" He hesitated momentarily. "Licensed private investigator," Bill said. And he looked again at the tall and dignified man, who presented a well-tailored back. "I wonder—" Bill did not finish. Instead he looked, and the others looked, at a short round man, red-tunicked, strapped in white webbing, wearing a white cap with a red band, who marched between the tables. As he marched, the scabbard of his gold-hilted sword tinkled against the legs of chairs. He looked very hot under his white cap and, Pam thought, slightly embarrassed. But he kept his eyes fixed straight ahead, and his plump shoulders back as well as he was able. The strain could be observed.

He marched—there was no other word for it—to the table over which Respected Captain Folsom presided. He stood where Folsom could see him, and stood at attention.

"Duty Officer Magumber reporting, sir," he said. "All present and accounted for, sir."

"Or, Magumber," Folsom said. "Present *or* accounted for."

"Sir," the man with the sword said.

"Carry on," Folsom said.

"Sir," the man with the sword said, and did an about-face. The sword swung with his movement; it banged into a shin of Respected Captain Folsom.

"Ouch!" Folsom said, in the aggrieved tones of a New England businessman of middle years. "Watch that damn' thing, Teddy."

"It was your idea, J.R.," Magumber said, in equally non-military tones. "Think I like lugging it around? Banging into things?"

"Officer of the Day, *carry on,*" Folsom said, reverting to Respected Captain.

"Sir," Theodore Magumber, of Theodore Magumber, Inc., Wholesale Produce, said, and went off, in a military manner, to carry on.

Jerry North choked slightly on his trifle.

"I think," Dorian said, as if she had been considering the question for some time, "that this is going to be a great deal of fun. I think the Ancient and Respectables will help."

"For short," Jerry told her, "they call themselves the Old Respectables."

"There will," the public-address system said, after a preliminary click, "be a cocktail party in the Coral Café this afternoon, to which all are invited. Thank you. Click." There was a momentary hush in the big room, in which upward of a hundred civilians and Old Respectables lunched, in which the lights were soft and the white-jacketed stewards quick. "Click," the public-address system said. "We are presently dropping the pilot. Thank you. Click."

A woman with improbably red hair went past the table for four at which Norths and Weigands toyed with trifle. Her movements were resolute, and somewhat more military than had been those of Officer of the Day Magumber. She was followed by a much younger woman with hair of no special color, who wore a linen suit, which had no special color either. The suit hung flatly, in straight lines.

The younger woman was, in turn, followed by the assistant chief steward, in a blue uniform. The red-haired woman, who was clearly in her sixties, the skin of whose face was tightly stretched and almost wrinkleless, stopped by a chair at Captain Folsom's table, and turned. She turned imperiously.

"Yes, Mrs. Macklin," the steward said, speaking quickly. "This is the captain's table, ma'am." He stepped around the thin youngish woman, and pulled out a chair for the woman with red hair. She looked sharply at Respected Captain Folsom, at J. Orville Marsh—who certainly, Pam thought, doesn't *look* like a private eye—and sat. The steward pulled out the chair on her right, and the thin young woman started to sit in it.

"Other side, man," Mrs. Macklin said, and her voice was sharp. *"Other* side. *You* ought to know, Hilda.". . .

It took all kinds to make a cruise, a fact upon which Pamela North commented some time later, standing with Jerry and Dorian in the swirl of a cocktail party in the café. Ancient and Respectable Riflemen in uniform (and not a few wearing their caps); staff captains; sharp-tongued, elderly women with improbably red hair. And, it was evident, a hundred or so more.

Among the kinds it also took was, most evidently, a hostess. She was a little tall, and just perceptibly angular, and what she wore Pam and Dorian, conferring by glance and, apparently, osmosis, considered a bit fussy. It was generally pinkish in hue, with blue accents at unexpected places, and it had perhaps been designed for a woman of whom there was more, here and there, than there was of Miss Springer.

"Now I am Miss Springer," she said, landing beside the Norths and Dorian like a friendly, if largish, bird. "I'm here to help everybody—*everybody*—have a good time. We must all *meet* people."

"Well," Pam said, "I'm Pamela North. This is my husband, Mr. North. This is Dorian Weigand." Pam paused momentarily. "Her husband's asleep," Pam said, feeling that she had left a gap. "He just arrested Killer McShane."

"What?" Miss Springer said. "Oh, of course. How nice."

"The killer didn't think it—" Pam began, with what sounded precisely like innocence. But Jerry looked at her. Jerry said he was sure they would all have a wonderful time. He said it was a very fine party.

It was. The waters through which the *Carib Queen* steamed were placid—she was a sparkling thing on a still sparkling sea. The setting sun danced into the starboard windows of the café lounge, on the sun-deck level, with french doors standing open to the after-deck, above the swimming pool. There was still a net over the swimming pool, which might, Pam thought, prove as well. Some of the Old Respectables—but one should not be censorious. The poor things, Pam thought. Their wives weren't with them. Only their rifles.

"Have you," Miss Springer said, "met Captain Smythe-Hornsby? I *know* he'll want to meet *you.* So *much."* She looked at them, blue eyes roundly bright; pinkened cheeks glowing with cordiality. *"Come,* dear people."

Unprotestingly, they went. Seen close, Captain Smythe-Hornsby was even younger, even more handsome, than he had seemed at table. Also, he was taller. He had changed to a white jacket. He was charmed at meeting Dorian Weigand, charmed anew at meeting Pamela North. Jerry's hand was taken in the firm clasp of friendship, and Jerry's eyes were looked forthrightly into. The captain was glad to have them all aboard and he hoped they were finding their way around our little ship. He hoped that they were, as he was, finding this little do a passable show.

"Oh, most," Dorian said. "Most charming."

"Quite," said Staff Captain Smythe-Hornsby. "Quite, Mrs.—" He hesitated. Dorian told him again.

"Silly ass," Captain Smythe-Hornsby said, apparently of himself. "Weigand, of course." He paused. "Of course," he said, "Weigand." And he spoke the name, the second time, as if it had a special meaning. "Hope the captain—" he said, but Miss Springer had returned. She had returned with the red-haired woman and, in the background, the girl with hair of no special color.

"You must, captain," Miss Springer said, with girl-ish enthusiasm over the treat in store, "you *must* let me introduce you to Mrs. Macklin. And her daughter, of course. Miss," she hesitated just perceptibly— "Macklin," she said, in triumph.

Captain Smythe-Hornsby was charmed. He hoped they were enjoying our little get-together.

Mrs. Macklin had very bright black eyes. She pointed them at the captain.

"There could," she said, in a high voice with a crack in it, "be more to drink."

She had something there, Pam North thought—not tact, certainly, but something. The stewards were doing all they could. That was evident. But there would always be more to drink at a party large as this. Waiters who seemed to be approaching were waylaid, wandered into bypaths. Or, quite simply, ran out of cocktails. But one did not—unless one were an Old Respectable or, apparently, a Mrs. Macklin—come to such parties as this to drink. One—

"Terribly sorry, you know," Captain Smythe-Hornsby said and then, in the tone of command, "Steward!" Instantly there was not merely a steward; there were stewards. Mrs. Macklin was supplied; so were the Norths and Dorian. Pale Hilda Macklin reached, or seemed to reach, toward the tray, but she withdrew her hand before the gesture was defined. "Nothing for me, thank you," she said, in a neat, pale voice.

"You may if you like," Mrs. Macklin said.

"Of course," Miss Macklin said. "Of course,

mother." But she shook her head and did not reach toward the tray.

"Then," Mrs. Macklin said, "I would appreciate your getting me a wrap. Or perhaps the knitted stole."

"Of course," the younger woman said, in the same pale voice, and went off through the crowded room, walking straight and stiff. Pam watched her oddly rigid progress, and watched with sympathy. To be so domineered over by a mother so much more formidable. From small things one could perceive their lives, Pam thought, doing so—the washed-out young woman, all her pale life at beck and call; afraid to take a drink, to rouge lips; squeezed dry by the imperious hands of a selfish mother; transfixed, as bird by snake, on the cold arrows of black eyes. And she can't, Pam thought, indignation growing, be older than the late twenties. No wonder the poor thing was straight up and down as a broom-handle, and with similar allure. How could she be expected to burgeon? How—

Having thus filled in the picture, Pam was surprised—was almost aggrieved—to see that, when she was near a door leading out of the lounge, Miss Macklin was intercepted. At least, she seemed to be intercepted, and by a man—by a man evidently young, darkly good-looking (almost Spanish, really) wearing a light sports jacket with noticeably wide shoulders, showing white teeth in a smile. Or—was she intercepted? Certainly it seemed that the man moved up to her, moved for a moment beside her. But it was less certain that Miss Macklin responded. Perhaps there was a slight motion of her head, but Pam could not be sure. And almost at once the young man moved aside and away, and Miss Macklin went on through the door which led her into a foyer with corridors running forward on either side of the ship.

If there had actually been a meeting, Pam thought, it had been oddly surreptitious. Lovers parted by circumstance, meeting for the briefest of words, of glances? Pam tried to think so. She remembered Hilda's pale face, her unrelenting straightness of outline under the meaningless linen suit, and abandoned the effort to think so. As Juliet, Miss Hilda Macklin simply wouldn't do.

"No, this will be the first time," Pam North said, catching a polite question by the tail when it was all but past her. "I'm sure we'll love Havana."

"Fascinating place," Captain Smythe-Hornsby told her. "Fine place to buy—" He was interrupted; Miss Springer had caught another, and brought him proudly. "I *know* you'll want to meet—" Miss Springer said, and offered Respected Captain Folsom—J. R. Folsom—still contained in red tunic and, it seemed to Pam somewhat unfortunately, wearing his cap. Captain Smythe-Hornsby did not, perhaps a little carefully did not, notice the cap. Or perhaps he thought cap-wearing in an enclosed place, while drinking cocktails, merely another curious American habit. He noticed the rest of the respected captain cordially.

It was then that Pam discovered she had at some stage—probably during her preoccupation with poor Hilda Macklin—been deserted by her husband and her devoted, green-eyed friend, Mrs. William Weigand. Of all things, Pam thought, and vanished from Captain Smythe-Hornsby's circle, leaving not even a smile behind. She found them. She found Bill with them—Bill and a tall, heavily handsome man who was—oh yes. A private eye. And who still did not accord with anything Pam knew of private eyes, admittedly almost nothing.

"So you tore yourself away," Jerry said, getting in first, and looking with meaning toward the handsome staff captain of the *Carib Queen*. "I'll have to get me a uniform."

"Do," Pam said. "You'd be cute as an Old Respectable."

With those formalities out of the way, she was introduced to Mr. J. Orville Marsh, whose dignity of speech proved to match his dignity of appearance. It seemed hardly possible.

"Are you really a private eye?" Pam North said, going to the point.

Marsh looked at Bill Weigand.

"Right," Bill said. "I did." Bill looked rested, now. He also looked somewhat amused.

"Yes," Marsh said to Pam. "At least, I used to be. Retired last year."

Pam was a little disappointed. It was bad luck to catch her first private eye just when it had closed.

"Do you call yourselves that, or is it like veterinarians?" Pam asked, then, and J. Orville Marsh looked gravely perplexed. He grasped the last word and repeated it, as one clinging to a final straw.

"Veterinarians?" he repeated. He blinked slightly. "Do we call ourselves veterinarians?"

"Private eyes," Pam said. "Or is it just something in books? Or is it like vets?" She had made it clear; she waited. Evidently, it was not clear. "Veterinarians," Pam said, "don't like to be called vets. But they call one another vets, when they're not thinking."

"Oh," Marsh said. "Yes, it is rather like that, Mrs.

North. Of course, the books—" He sighed; he looked at Bill Weigand.

Bill continued to look mildly amused.

"Most of my work," Marsh said, in the tone of one who has often said much the same thing, "was concerned with missing persons. A good deal of it was done by telephone—we merely called people up and—er, asked them about other people. When the occasion arose, we co-operated fully with the authorities." He nodded toward Bill Weigand, indicating one of them. "I never carried a gun in my life," he added, and then he smiled. But he had, Pam thought, a careful smile. "I'm afraid it's a little disillusioning," J. Orville Marsh said.

"Not even wire-tapping?" Pam asked.

Marsh looked at Weigand. He looked away again. "Only," he said firmly, "in co-operation with the authorities. Always—"

But he stopped then, as if his interest had flagged suddenly. He looked away from them and around the room. He could, Pam thought, see more than most, being taller than most. She wondered what had distracted him, but, being by no means taller than most, she could not see.

Marsh, it appeared, followed movement with his eyes, his head moving too. Then, at a door leading out to the sun deck, Pam saw what he appeared to be looking at. But it was merely the departure of Mrs. Macklin, preceding her daughter. Mrs. Macklin wore a white knitted stole. It was true that they seemed to be in a hurry, but that did not really make them very interesting.

"Well, nice to have met you," J. Orville Marsh said. "See you again." He went, with that. He did not, however, go in the direction the Macklins had gone.

He went through a door leading forward into the ship.

"I," Jerry North said, "know a better 'ole. One we can sit in."

He led them to it—the smoking room forward, where they could sit in comfortable seats, and be brought drinks made to order. There were some Old Respectables there, to be sure, and twice the officer of the day marched through, his sword dangling. (Magumber had been relieved of duty; the new OD was balder.) After a time four of the Old Respectables began to sing, but the loud-speaker spoke through the first verse, offering dinner to second sitters.

The only really jarring note came as they left. At a small table near the door, Mrs. Macklin was sitting, her red hair, which had been before neat if improbable, dangling low in disorder. Mrs. Macklin was alone. She appeared to be quite drunk. She was a spectacle to dampen gaiety, and she did.

2

The morning sparkled and, although they had over-night steamed only a part of the way down the Atlantic coast, it was already very warm. But sunny October days are seldom cold, particularly if one slips southward, carefree, in a small bright ship. The thought that there is, for some days, nothing one can conceivably do about anything is in itself warming. And the swimming pool had been filled. The water in it sparkled under the sun.

Bill Weigand could not, Pam thought, approaching, be said to sparkle. He seemed, indeed, to be asleep in one of the four deck chairs, labeled "North" and "Weigand," two by two. The apprehension of Killer McShane had, evidently, been a tiring business. Pam, wearing a bathing suit under a terry-cloth robe, carry-ing a bottle of sun-tan oil, approached more or less on tiptoe. But Bill twitched, indicating he might stand up if anything so absurd were insisted upon, and he said, "Hello." He even turned his head to look at Pam, who perched on the next deck chair and considered the exertion of applying oil to moderately browned legs—

and so forth. The bathing suit left a good deal of and so forth, and Jerry liked it very much. Pam decided to rest for a time, before applying oil. After all, she had walked from their cabin, amidships. There was no need to rush things.

"Dorian's changing," Bill said, in a sleepy voice. "Yours?"

"Walking," Pam said. "Around and around. So many laps to so much, you know. He'll probably be by any minute." She paused. She looked at the sparkling pool, and put on sunglasses. Bill already wore them—sunglasses and polo shirt and Bermuda shorts. He looked entirely unlike a captain of detectives, assigned to Homicide, Manhattan West. But then, he never did, particularly. "Do you suppose he's going to go athletic on me? After all this time?"

" 'You will find yourself invigorated by sea air,' " Bill said, in the tone of one who quotes. "Probably it will wear off."

Gerald North, not looking particularly like a book publisher, rounded into sight, doing a steady three and a half knots. He wore a sports shirt about which Pam was a little doubtful, and slacks—the kind of slacks one could wash out and hang up, and wear unpressed when dry. Jerry was slightly flushed, but almost ostentatiously bright of eye. He lifted a hand to sluggards and rounded out of sight.

"It doesn't seem to be," Pam said, beginning to rub in oil. "Is he really retired?"

Bill boarded her train of thought with the ease of one who has had long practice. He said that he didn't know; that he had not heard of it. But that there was no reason he should have heard. If J. Orville Marsh said he was retired, probably he was retired.

"Not coming the innocent on us?" Pam asked,

remembering that the *Carib Queen* was, after all, of British registry. "Lurking? Planning to pounce on malefactors?"

J. Orville was not, Bill told her, of the pouncing type. He was—or had been—what he said: a specialist in the seeking out of missing persons. Now and then, he made discreet investigations on the instructions of, for example, corporations which had grown doubtful of highly placed employees, but preferred not to go out on limbs about it. If it became a matter for the authorities, J. Orville made the correct contacts.

"A completely clean slate?" Pam said, in a voice a little tinged with disappointment. She began to oil her right leg, having finished with the left. Bill nodded, but without lifting his head. "Why not the Missing Persons Bureau?" Pam asked. She found that, already, she was getting sleepy. But she had come for an invigorating dip.

"Because sometimes people want to keep things in families," Bill told her. "When we move in, officially, a good many people get involved. Necessarily. And sometimes there's no legal justification for searching people out and—" It appeared that the subject tired him. Or that he felt it finished. McShane must, Pam thought, have been *extremely* hard to come up with.

There were at first only a dozen or so around the pool, and only two in it—a blond young woman with a blond young boy. But more came. Mrs. Macklin came. Mrs. Macklin wore a wide straw hat. She wore sunglasses, and a green wrap. She stood and looked at chairs, and at the sun, and at the other people, and at chairs again. Hilda Macklin came after her, carrying things—a large bag, towels, several magazines and a thermos bottle.

"Here," Mrs. Macklin said and selected a chair on the edge of the North-Weigand reservation. "This will have to do."

Her voice was high; there was still a crack in it. In the sunlight, her skin seemed to fit more tightly than ever on her bones. Hilda Macklin unloaded on the chair next the one Mrs. Macklin indicated. Hilda wore a loose robe over, presumably, a bathing suit—at any rate, slim legs were visible below the robe. She bent and looked at the tag on the chair.

"I'm afraid," she said, in a low and colorless voice, "that this one belongs to someone. A Mr.—Folsóm."

"Don't be absurd," Mrs. Macklin said. "There are plenty of chairs, as anyone can see." She sat in Mr.— in Respected Captain—Folsom's chair. She slightly parted the green wrap. Under it she wore a pink sports dress, very short on elderly white legs; quarreling in color with the red hair, all but a little of which was concealed by the wide hat.

Pam North oiled her left arm and shoulder.

"Well," Mrs. Macklin said, in the same high voice, "go if you're going."

Hilda Macklin slipped out of the shapeless robe. Under it, she wore a bathing suit—an unexpectedly sleek bathing suit. And—well, for goodness' sake! Pam thought. Who would have thought it? She looked at Hilda Macklin with generous surprise.

Hilda Macklin, peeled out of linen suit, of loose-hanging robe, was by no means the shape of a broomstick. She was slender, not thin. Nowhere did she lack anything it was appropriate for her to have—from slender high-arched feet upward. Hilda walked toward the deep end of the pool. Unencumbered, she moved with fluid grace—moved, Pam thought, almost as

Dorian moved. She poised on the pool's rim, her arms lifted, the position lifting small and perfect breasts. She dove, cutting cleanly into the sparkling water.

"Appearances deceive," Bill Weigand said, softly, from the chair beside Pam's. He was still lying relaxed, but it was quite evident he was not asleep.

"But," Pam said, as softly, "why? Why hide them under a bushel?"

Bill had no answer. Jerry rounded into sight again. He wasn't now, Pam thought, doing better than three knots. He flicked a hand, however, and rounded out of sight.

"Once more, and we get him to keep," Pam told Bill Weigand, and then Dorian came along the deck—came with almost a cat's matchless grace. She wore a green swim suit darker than her eyes, and a short white jacket. She sat next Pam. She oiled. When she was ready, she said, "Well?" and Pam went with her to the pool, and into it. They came out, in time, and toweled, and Hilda Macklin remained, darting like a fish among half a dozen others in the water. Jerry was sitting next to Bill. Questioned, he claimed two miles, not one.

There were now a good many people around the pool, and white-jacketed stewards began to move among them. Mrs. Macklin beckoned with decision; she was, in time, brought a drink deeply red, and downed it in two swallows. "Bloody Mary," Pam said, "and I should think she'd need it." They relaxed in the sun, and watched through dark glasses, and as the sun grew higher—and hotter—spoke less.

Respected Captain Folsom came and peered at Mrs. Macklin, in his chair. The respected captain wore pink slacks and a mottled shirt, and tennis shoes. And his uniform cap. Observed by Pam, he nodded to her, and then, when Jerry said, "Good morning, captain," he came to stand above Jerry. He said it was a swell day. He hoped they were having a swell time.

"Where's your officer of the day?" Jerry asked him, in lazy tones, keeping things going. "Walking his post in a military manner?"

"Well," Folsom said, "the fact is, one of the boys is up to tricks. Great little joke, one of the boys pulled. Hidden the sword." He made a sound like laughter. "Swallowed it, maybe," he said. "Some of the boys will swallow anything."

"Why?" Pam asked. "What would be the point of it?"

"Bangs into things," Folsom said. "I don't deny that. But, damn it all—I'm sorry, ladies—darn it all, it's an *emblem*. See what I mean?" He looked at them, and now there seemed to be anxiety in his ruddy face. "Part of the whole thing," he explained. "Keeps up the *standard* of the whole thing. Just because it bangs into things—after all, nobody's got the duty for more than an hour at a stretch."

"You rotate?" Dorian said. "All of you?"

"All but me," Folsom said. "And the adjutant. He locks things up at night. Counts and locks up. Can't have weapons around loose." He looked at them severely. "Those are real rifles," he told them.

"Real sword, too?" Pam asked him, and there was only polite interest in her voice.

"Sure," Folsom said, and then looked at them again, and it seemed—to Pam at any rate—that there was something almost wistful in his expression. "All right," he said, "suppose it looks silly? *We* like it. We spend fifty weeks a year in offices and making contacts and what have you." He looked particularly at Jerry North. "You get out with the boys," he told Jerry. "Like anybody else."

"Sure," said Jerry, who had found that getting out with the boys was for the most part a tedious business, but who knew better than to admit, publicly, so un-American an attitude.

"Captain Folsom," Pam said. "It isn't silly at all. Nobody thinks it is. It's just swe—I mean, sort of gay and jolly."

"The wife thinks it's silly," Folsom said. "I keep telling her—"

But an Old Respectable, in full uniform—but sword-less—came to stand at attention before the respected captain, and to make an elaborate motion with his head. Folsom said, "Excuse me, folks," and went away with the—diminished, unemblemed—officer of the day.

"I wouldn't have expected him—" Pam began, and was interrupted by the public-address system, which clicked clear its metallic throat and continued: "Will the following please communicate with the purser? Mr. or Mrs. Oscar Peterson. Mr. or Mrs. Gerald North. Captain or Mrs. William Weigand. Mr.—er Captain—J. R. Folsom. Thank you. Click."

It is disconcerting to have one's name called over a public-address system—bandied, as Pam thought of it—before the many passengers of a ship. It leads, or led with Pam, to an unaccountable sense of guilt.

"Oh," Pam said, "I wonder what we've done wrong?" She paused. Her eyes widened. "Do you suppose we're on the wrong ship?" she asked the others. "Do something, Jerry," she told Jerry, who looked at Bill Weigand, and Dorian, for alternative suggestions. "Just inside," Dorian said. "A desk. Says 'Purser' on it."

Jerry said, "Oh, all right," and got up and went.

"Whatever in the—" Pam said, and did not finish.

She was distracted; Hilda Macklin, who had long been in it, was coming sleek and glistening from the pool. She certainly had been wrong about Miss Macklin, Pam thought again. Why would she hide all that? Her mother, of course. Pam looked at Mrs. Macklin with disapproval. Mrs. Macklin's black eyes were hidden by her sunglasses; possibly she was asleep.

A darkly good-looking young man, in swimming trunks—a young man deeply browned, with extremely white teeth in a dark face—got up from a deck chair near the pool and started to walk among the chairs. His path intersected that of Hilda Macklin, bound away from the pool. He was—Pam was almost sure he was—the handsome young man who had (but had he really?) intercepted Hilda briefly, inconclusively, at the cocktail party. Now he was—

But he was not; it was clear he was not. He stopped to let Hilda pass and now they were close enough to her for Pam to be sure that no sign of recognition passed between them. So—she had been wrong about that, also. It was more a pity than ever, now that Miss Macklin, viewed more fully, could very well do as Juliet. With, of course, a little lipstick. She and the dark young man, whose swimming trunks were white, would make a very nice-looking couple.

Jerry North reappeared. His face was serious. It took even Pam a moment to realize that the seriousness was too heavily laid on. It was not like Jerry to shake his head dolefully; he should know it was not like him. But he managed a few portentous words. "It seems we've made a—" Jerry began, in a voice of moderate gloom. Pam looked at him.

"All right," Jerry said. "Captain Cunningham's compliments, and he would be pleased if we could join him for cocktails in his cabin before lunch. One-ish, the purser said. I said it sounded like a jolly-ish sort of do."

"You didn't," Dorian said. "I surely hope you didn't. 'Jolly-ish,' indeed."

"I said we'd be glad to," Jerry said. "Taking it upon myself."

"Cunningham?" Pam said, and answered her own question. There were information brochures in the cabins; Pam had read hers. "Oh," she said. "The real captain. Captain Peter Cunningham, RNR."

Jerry agreed that it was the real captain.

"You'll have to change your shirt," Pam told him. . . .

They had all changed their shirts, or the equivalents, when they went, one-ish, for cocktails with the captain (the real captain) of the *Carib Queen*. From the level of the sun deck, they went upward in an elevator labeled "Lift" and were released into a small foyer, where the captain's steward met them. The captain's steward was a rosy youth, immaculately white as to jacket. He ushered them up a short flight of steel stairs and into the quarters of Captain Peter Cunningham. And Captain Cunningham was as real a captain as anyone could wish.

He was tall and lean and unassertively British. He had a long, tanned face and steady blue eyes; he was, Pam decided, precisely what Noel Coward had years before had in mind in that Navy picture during which Mr. Coward spent so much time under water. Captain Cunningham welcomed them to the most ship-shape of small sitting rooms. He was gravely cordial; if this mingling with selected passengers—and how, Pam wondered, selected—was in any sense a matter of duty, nothing in Captain Cunningham's manner suggested that there were other things he would rather be doing.

Pam and Jerry, Dorian and Bill, were first, but only by minutes. Respected Captain J. R. Folsom was next, and now he was in full uniform, complete with cap. A little unexpectedly, once in the cabin, Folsom stood to attention and saluted, as one officer to another. Pam looked for surprise on Captain Cunningham's long face, and found none—found only grave courtesy. Captain Cunningham even returned the salute, although uncovered. Courtesy could hardly go further.

The rosy steward—beamish if anyone ever was— served cocktails and canapés. The canapés were admirable, the drinks cold and as ordered. Captain Cunningham sipped sherry and they talked tentatively as people do, when met at cocktail parties. The room was small enough to be talked across, and the captain, who was clearly experienced in such matters, prompted conversation. And he seemed to listen to everyone, and to listen as if he heard.

This was true even after Mr. and Mrs. Oscar Peterson arrived, to fill the small, neat room. Mr. Peterson was short and round, and wore a gray business suit— unexpectedly complete with vest. His wife was a little larger, but of the same general design; she wore a flowery print. Mr. Peterson operated a flour mill in Minnesota; it was the first time they had been on what Mrs. Peterson preferred to think of as a boat. And about this lack of wide experience they were in no way defensive. Some people lived in New York and went to night clubs (Mrs. Peterson didn't doubt) and others were captains of cruise ships; some published books (apparently) and others milled flour. It was the way things should be, and nobody made a point of "living up" to anyone else—or even, Pam realized, thought of doing so. Mr. and Mrs. Peterson were very sweet, and Mr. Peterson was interesting on the subject of flour. It had never occurred to Pamela North that flour could be so interesting, and she got some very good advice from Mary Peterson about the making of cherry pie.

In civilian life, Respected Captain Folsom made shoe boxes—paper boxes in general, but shoe boxes in particular. This momentarily surprised Pamela North, for reasons slightly obscure. Once thought of, it became evident that somebody—and Mr. Folsom as well as any—had to make shoe boxes; clearly boxes did not merely grow around shoes, as cocoons about larvae. Pam had merely never thought of it before. When you came to think of it, as Pam now did, somebody had to make rubber bands, too. The world is a varied place.

The minds of Mr. Peterson and Mr. Folsom met briefly—one of these days the unions were going to go too far; not that they disapproved of unions, but—and were parted by Mrs. Peterson, who had the air of a person who had certainly heard that one before. Mrs. Peterson parted them by complimenting Respected Captain Folsom on his uniform. She had, she said, never seen a uniform quite like it. Pam looked at her, and decided that Mrs. Peterson meant it in only the nicest way.

"Traditional," Folsom told them. "Been the same since the Riflemen were organized. War of 1812, you know. Stood by to repel those damned—" He stopped, abruptly.

"Quite all right," Captain Cunningham said. "Threw our weight around a bit, probably."

"Er—"Folsom said. "Anyway, been going on ever since. Drills. Kind of a militia. Not that it *is* the militia. I don't say that. Have a dinner once a month and when something comes up people ought to take a stand on, we take a stand on it. Know what I mean?"

Pam was a little afraid she did. But she smiled

brightly, at the same time warning Jerry with a quick glance. He smiled reassurance; he would not go into the matter of stands taken. One of them would probably turn out to be on books permissible to libraries, but this was vacation.

"Very interesting," Captain Cunningham said. (The place was certainly, Pam thought, full of captains, especially if one counted Bill, as she supposed one had to.)

"Have you," Dorian asked, "found the sword?"

Somewhat gloomily, Folsom shook his head—from which he had, as an afterthought, removed his cap.

"Sword?" Captain Cunningham said. The Petersons merely looked puzzled. "Oh, of course," Cunningham said. "Officer of the deck's sword."

"Day," Folsom said. "Officer of the day."

"Much the same thing," Cunningham said. "You've lost it? On the ship? Job for you there, Weigand. Your line of country, what?"

"Not," Bill said, "unless it's found on somebody. More J. Orville's."

The ship's captain, and the Old Respectables' captain looked blank at that, and the Petersons politely puzzled. Briefly, Bill explained J. Orville Marsh. Recognition dawned on Captain Cunningham's long face.

"Matter of fact," he said, "got him on my list, I think. That is—" He stopped.

"But of course, captain," Pam said. "There would have to be a list. Because if you'd picked just anywhere, we wouldn't have come in a—a set, would we?" She looked hopefully at Captain Cunningham. He looked hopefully back. "Bill and Dorian," Pam said. "Jerry and me. We must have been in a bracket on your list."

"Oh," Cunningham said. "As a matter of fact, yes.

Comes from the head office, the list does. Special people the directors want to—er, honor. Awkward word for it, but there you are." He paused. "Or," he said, *"here* you are. Mrs. North could do with a cocktail, Cholly." Cholly was the beamish boy; Cholly brought drinks. "One of the pleasures of my trade, as a matter of fact," the captain said. He sipped sherry. He was still on his first glass, and the glass was still almost full.

"Missing persons, eh?" Folsom said, and seemed much interested. "That all he does?"

"Did, he tells me," Bill said. "No. Some corporation work. Employee investigation. That sort of thing. Shortages which aren't clear enough to sign complaints, for example. You still think one of the—one of your organization—hid the sword? So, I gather, as not to have to wear it?"

For a moment, it appeared that Respected Captain Folsom was thinking of something else.

"Oh," Folsom said, returning. "Sure—that's all it could be. Seems Jonesy forgot to lock up last night. The gun cases, that is. Jonesy's the adjutant. Slipped his mind, what with one thing and another. So he doesn't know if it was in. Old Riggsy says he put it there and he had the last tour. But—there you are."

It was not entirely clear where they were. Bill Weigand is a man who likes things clear: Pam could see the desire for clarity flicker briefly in his eyes.

"Vacation, darling," Dorian said from the deep chair in which she was sitting, a foot tucked under her. "Remember?"

"Right," Bill said.

"It'll turn up," Folsom said. "Always does. About this private detective, does—"

Somebody knocked rather loudly at the door of the

captain's quarters. Cholly came out of the captain's sleeping cabin, in temporary use as a serving pantry, and went to the door and opened it. Mrs. Macklin, her red hair neat again, but wearing a green dress, came in at once, brushing past the steward.

"I am Mrs. Macklin," she said, speaking to Captain Cunningham; ignoring the others. "I am seated at your table."

She spoke loudly, in her high voice, and the voice cracked. There was a kind of violence in the elderly woman, with the skin drawn to such unnatural tightness over the bones of her face.

"I demand you do something," she said.

She was not a large woman and was of what Pam always thought of as the top-heavy type, believing that almost all women incline either to top- or bottom-heaviness. But, standing in the middle of the room, looking up at the tall ship's captain, Mrs. Macklin seemed to fill the room.

"Certainly," Captain Cunningham said. "Whatever I can. But—about what?"

"I supposed," she said, "that this would be a well-run ship. I was assured it would prove a well-run ship."

She spoke distinctly; although the ship moved a little on the quiet sea, she did not sway. And yet it was evident that, again, she had drunk more than she had been wise to drink.

"It is," Captain Cunningham said, simply, with patience. "You have something to complain of?"

"Complain of?" she said. "Complain of indeed! Somebody in my room last night. After dinner. Went over everything. Your well-run ship! A thieving steward."

"Our people are carefully selected," Captain Cunningham said, and was entirely formal, although there was frost on his voice. "You make a serious charge, Mrs. Macklin. What was stolen?"

"Stolen?" she said. "Nothing stolen. Probably heard me coming. Nosing around. Looking."

"Probably," Cunningham said, "the stewardess straightened up. That's her job."

"You think I don't know?" Mrs. Macklin said, and her voice was higher than before. "Think I can't tell?"

Quite clearly, the captain did.

"Precisely what—" he began, and she interrupted.

"As bad as the rest," she said. "This purser of yours. This other captain."

"Oh," Cunningham said. "You've seen the purser? Captain Smythe-Hornsby? I'm sure they're doing everything that can be done, Mrs. Macklin."

Captain Cunningham spoke calmly, seriously; standing tall and competent, he epitomized reassurance. Nor was there anything in his manner to indicate that he did not take Mrs. Macklin as seriously as she could wish. And yet it was as if his quiet words had touched a trigger.

Violence in the aging woman had been evident until then, but it had been restrained. But then all restraint vanished—then as if there had been some explosion inside her, Mrs. Macklin began to scream—at the captain, at all of them. Her words—her screamed words—lost coherence; the tightly stretched skin of her face became red and mottled.

Captain Cunningham was against her, like the rest. She screamed at him—"You don't care. Nobody—" She had a right to protection—she—"Kill me in my bed," she screamed at him, and turned to the others.

"All of you!" she said. "Laughing—laughing—they'll kill me." She became momentarily obscene. She seemed to hear her own words. "Don't say those things," she said. "You hear me? Don't—" She moved toward the captain, as if to claw at his unchanging face.

It was something—it was a drunken outburst—from which one wanted to get away—something from which one wanted to run away. At first no one moved. Then Peter Cunningham moved. He stretched out strong hands and grasped the woman's shoulders. He held her, for a moment, saying nothing.

And, held so, she at once stopped her screamed, inarticulate tirade. She stood quietly; then she said, "What did you say?"

Captain Cunningham said nothing. He merely looked at her.

"I'm afraid," Mrs. Macklin said, quite calmly, "that I allowed myself to get a little excited."

You could have laughed at that. Nobody laughed.

"Can't I offer you a drink?" Captain Cunningham asked her, as a host asks a guest.

"Why, thank you," she said. "Thank you. A little bourbon and water, perhaps. But, very little bourbon, please."

"Cholly," Captain Cunningham said, and Cholly hurried. He was back almost at once, with a glass. He no longer looked beamish. He looked embarrassed.

"Thank you so much," Mrs. Macklin said, and took the glass, and held it daintily and raised it to her lips— and without pause drank half of it. "As to the little matter I bothered you with—" she said, and raised the glass to her lips again.

There were melodious chimes; a gently spoken, if

metallically spoken, announcement from everywhere that the second luncheon sitting was prepared.

They went. It was by the exercise of considerable restraint that they did not jostle one another at the door. Mrs. Macklin did, indeed, dampen gaiety. She was almost, Pam thought, enough to make one give up alcohol.

3

Aboard the *Carib Queen,* cruising south in smooth seas, there were many things that one could do to pass the pleasant time. As Miss Springer said, there was always *some*thing going on. (But on the other hand, there was certainly no com*pul*sion.) One could swim in the sparkling pool; one could attend a movie in the air-conditioned theater forward. One could walk around the decks; in the air-conditioned smoking room, one could participate in a bridge tournament. In the forward lounge one could, at the appropriate time, partake of tea. If one were a member of the Ancient and Respectable Riflemen, one could attend a special cocktail party which the Ancient and Respectables were giving themselves. There would be—and indeed there was—horseracing by the swimming pool. On the boat deck, one might play shuffleboard or deck tennis. And all this was only during the afternoon; after dinner there would be further enticements, including dancing, including the antics of "famous Broadway entertainers."

But it is one of the other pleasures of a cruise, during

which one relaxes like a jelly in the sun, that none of these things need be done. It is agreeable to think that so many presumably pleasant activities are available; that perhaps tomorrow they will be availed of. But there is no hurry. As Pamela North summed it up, at luncheon, nobody was going anywhere and, although the *Carib Queen* herself clearly was, if in no great hurry, Pam's statement was unchallenged. Also, the lunch was ample, and they found themselves hungry. The sea *air* as Miss Springer was accustomed to say.

They could eat and look about them idly, and this they did. Mrs. Macklin and Miss Macklin appeared, somewhat late, at the captain's table. Miss Macklin was back in her colorless suit; Mrs. Macklin seemed to have made a quick, if perhaps partial, recovery. She ate her luncheon like a lady. Respected Captain Folsom ate his like a rifleman. J. Orville Marsh was even later than the Macklins, and smiled affably at the Norths and the Weigands as he passed their table. Captain Peter Cunningham did not appear to preside. The first officer substituted, from the foot of the table. Mr. and Mrs. Oscar Peterson, who before had been only blurs, were discovered at the staff captain's table, and smiled and nodded across it as eyes were caught.

Not so many of the Old Respectables were now in uniform. Some seemed to be shedding it gradually—a jacket replacing tunic, but the uniform trousers remaining in their place. (One of them did, to be sure, wear his tunic, with Bermuda shorts.) Not nearly so many wore their caps to lunch; it was possible that word had been passed. The officer of the day made two appearances on his rounds, and wore no sword. He did, however, wear white gloves as compensation. The apple tart looked naice today and, within reason, was. Having tried coffee the night before, Pam essayed the tea. Jerry was of sterner stuff and said so; he would fight on the coffee line if it took all cruise.

The four drifted apart after luncheon. Confronted by entertainment unlimited, Bill Weigand decided to take a nap. Dorian went to the boat deck, with drawing pad and pencils, since the holidays of commercial artists are likely to be a little like those of busmen.

Jerry North, after having changed his shirt again, and resumed the slacks which did not need pressing, made one circuit of the promenade deck—but at not over two knots—and joined Pamela, who was merely sitting. She had changed back to a bathing suit, but this time only for tanning purposes. They sat contentedly, saying little, toasting slowly. The bow of the ship rose lazily; it subsided dreamily and the stern apathetically arose. "It's wonderful to have nothing—nothing at all—to do," Pam said, at one point, and Jerry said, "M-mm" in agreement, since a sound was simpler to come by than a word. "I suppose," Pam said, some time later, "I really ought to go into the pool." Jerry said, "M-mm" again. "Probably you're right," Pam said. "Take things easy to start with."

Respected Captain Folsom was, presumably, at the Respectables' cocktail party; Mrs. Macklin did not appear—it could, by one with that kind of mind, be assumed that she was drinking in her cabin. (And that's the kind of mind I've got, Pam admitted to herself.) Hilda Macklin did not appear; possibly she was also in the cabin, pouring. Captain Cunningham probably was at the wheel, peering from it into the distance. It was comforting to know that they were in strong hands. Nothing untoward could happen; ahead stretched days of peace. Pam North dozed in the sun.

Aboard a cruise ship one can attend a movie, or play shuffleboard or doze in the sun. But it is inevitable that, as time goes on, one will sit at a table in the smoking lounge, and there prepare, in the only proper fashion, for the subsequent consumption of further food. The Norths do not contend against the inevitable.

At a quarter of six, when the inevitable caught up with them, Pam wore a white dinner dress—and wished, mildly, that its décolletage coincided more exactly with that of her bathing suit. Even with oil, one reddens in the sun. Jerry had changed his shirt again— he wore a white dinner jacket and black trousers and even a cummerbund, and a dress shirt which would dry overnight and did not need pressing. They sat, at a table which would accommodate four, and was expected to, and began to prepare for dinner. The bartender made admirable martinis; it was clear he was American trained.

Bill Weigand and Dorian were tardy. But the Norths were only started on their drinks when J. Orville Marsh appeared, also wearing a white dinner jacket, tall and heavily handsome—a man of distinction, bound toward a drink before dinner. He nodded his gray head, and smiled pleasantly and said, "Good evening," and was about to pass on.

"Join us," Jerry said, to Pam's surprise.

Mr. Marsh said, "Why, thank you," and that he didn't mind if he did. He did.

"Talking about you before lunch," Jerry said, when Marsh had ordered. "Seems the Old Respectables have lost their sword. Case of the missing weapon."

"Oh," Marsh said. "Of me?" His drink came. He had ordered a daiquiri. He sipped it. "Oh," he said. "I see." He was, Pam thought, content to let it lie there. But Jerry was not—

Talk about busmen's holidays, Pam thought, although nobody had been. Publishers are just the same, the dears. Looking for books in the oddest places.

But as J. Orville Marsh was led on—and once started he led easily—and as Bill and Dorian still tarried (gone to sleep, probably) Pam began to doubt whether Mr. Marsh was really the oddest place. Mr. Marsh told stories, and he told them well. He had never, to be sure, carried a gun. He had never shot a man, or been shot at. Murder was, naturally, not his line. He had never happened to run into a private investigator whose line it was. But people disappeared under odd circumstances, and sometimes with odd completeness. There was the man who, three years before, had taken his own two children, after a quarrel with his wife, got with them onto a bus and vanished from the face of the earth. "Difficult with kids," Mr. Marsh said. And there was the wealthy woman who had turned somewhat peculiar and similarly vanished, leaving worried children. There was—there was always—Judge Crater who had been, Marsh was almost certain, alive several years after he had vanished, although there was another theory about that. There was the man found, after an absence of two years, during an afternoon when Marsh had not left his office, and had made not quite a hundred telephone calls.

Mr. Marsh was by no means boastful, or so it seemed to Pam. When he said, "Edgar called me about that," it was unnecessary to believe that Edgar had not. Led to it—yes, there was a good deal of wiretapping; not so much as some people said, probably more than there should be. One trouble with wiretapping was that, in getting what you wanted—and not always getting that—you got, in addition, a great deal of information which was none of your business—which wasn't too bad, if you were scrupulous, which it could not be argued everybody was.

But, although he had carried on—"before I retired," Mr. Marsh made a point of saying; several times made a point of saying—a variety of investigations, he had been concerned mostly with those people who vanished. A former actress, for example—now here, now nowhere; traced finally to a hotel room where she seemed to be under the rather strange control of a lawyer and a practical nurse. And where, which was the trouble, she was firm she would remain. Mr. Marsh, who didn't like the situation—the former actress had had a good deal of money once—had thought of going to the authorities on that one but—He shrugged. There was nothing to pin on anyone, nothing tangible to get hold of. No law had been openly transgressed, and there was no one to make complaint.

"Of course," he said, "that is our only excuse for existence. To investigate—" He apparently sought a word. "Oddities," he said. "Matters which concern individuals, not society. Matters which need a kind of discretion the authorities can't, of course, promise. And—negotiations, of course. For the—well, the return of money, say. Amicable settlements. Not against the law, of course. But, say, beside the law. And—"

Dorian and Bill Weigand arrived, then. Dorian wore a gray dinner dress; she moved down the room, ahead of Bill, with that singular grace which always made Pam think of a cat's grace. The cat named Gin, for example, walked in much the same fashion, if one took additional legs into account. It must, Pam thought, be something about the way Dorian's put together. Bill, who looked rested, finally, wore a white dinner jacket.

(I wish they'd wear them all the time, Pam thought.) "We're ahead of you," Pam said, as Jerry and Marsh stood up.

The dignified licensed investigator—it was flatly impossible to think of him as a "private eye," although Pam tried to—remained for another drink; insisted, indeed, on buying drinks around. Then, unhurriedly, he got up, said it had been very pleasant, and went toward the bar.

"Jerry's been looking for a book," Pam said, to Dorian and Bill. "You think he is?" she said to Jerry, who shrugged, who said, "Could be."

The big lounge filled with second sitters, preparing themselves. The bar, which ran along one bulkhead, became lined with Old Respectables, who were he-men and drank standing. They were not, now, in all cases distinguishable by uniforms, or even parts of uniforms. A few retained regalia, complete to cap. But others, in dinner jackets, in business suits, were recognizable only by what Pam, reverting to the nautical, called "the cut of their jib."

"In other words," Jerry said, "middle-aged businessmen on convention."

Pam supposed so. If one wanted to make things easy. "Although," she said, "with rifles."

The steward who had been serving them approached, although he had not been summoned. He said, "Captain Folsom's compliments, and he would be 'appy to buy you drinks."

They looked toward the bar. J. Orville Marsh and Respected Captain Folsom stood there side by side. Folsom, who remained in uniform, but wore a white shirt and a black bow tie, smiled at them, and nodded vigorously.

"Thank Captain Folsom very much for us," Jerry said, and they all beamed in the respected captain's direction.

"In Nassau," Bill said, "they're going to parade. Hence the armament. They are going to present something to the governor general—a plaque of some kind—as a token of international friendship."

They looked at him.

"That's all I know," Bill said.

"In this form," Dorian told him, "it is a somewhat barren bit of knowledge."

Bill grinned at her. He said he was sorry. He told her it was all he had to offer.

"And you a detective," Dorian said, sadly, and the steward brought their complimentary drinks. They raised glasses toward the respected captain, who raised his in return.

They sipped, and awaited summoning chimes. The chimes sounded and, after a decent interval—they preferred not to clamor at the doors—they left the pleasant air-cooled place and went aft through passageways. It was only then that they noticed increased motion in the ship. She still rocked gently fore and aft; now also she rolled amiably port to starboard. The corridor bulkheads had a mild tendency to push at those who walked between them. It would, Pam said, give the Old Reliables, or such as needed it, an excuse for any untoward movements.

Captain Cunningham, in a white mess jacket, for the first time presided at his table—a table for the captain, the first officer and eight selected passengers. How selected? Pam wondered, and decided that for them, also, there must be a list. Possibly the pleasant young couple—perhaps from Kansas—on the captain's right were starting their married life on the *Carib Queen*. They looked as if they might be. She hoped the young man would continue to like his wife in that particular shade of blue. The couple on the captain's left were, almost certainly, retired—now that all their children were married, their grandchildren clustering—and taking their ease in a ship. They had had, Pam thought, at least three children—two boys and a girl. The woman wore a soft gray dress and orchids were pinned to it—of course! A wedding anniversary trip. How nice—how nice, indeed, everything was.

Respected Captain Folsom sat next the man who had brought his wife orchids for their anniversary. (How different, Pam thought, some men were from Jerry.) Marsh, a little late, sat next Folsom. They needed better assortment; they did not come properly two by two. It would have been easy to arrange, since Mrs. Macklin and her daughter sat across the table from Folsom and Marsh. They could have been split.

It was true that, this evening, they were not both there to split. Hilda was, in a dinner dress which seemed not so much to have been designed as to have happened. Mrs. Macklin was not. Pam, resolutely, decided to be charitable. No doubt the motion of the ship had diminished her appetite—for food at any rate.

"It would be pleasant," Jerry said, gently, "if you would make up your mind which table you're sitting at. The man says the roast beef looks very naice this evening."

They ate. They sat on the afterdeck, enjoying the cradling motion of the ship. They danced, later, and then the cradling movement was less desirable; Pam found herself always backing downhill, which seemed obscurely unfair. The anniversary couple danced, gently, once; the honeymooning couple danced briskly, often. The dark young man danced with a blond young woman, and they both danced noticeably well.

Elsewhere in the ship work was done. A seaman stood at the wheel; the second officer got a fix, moved parallel rulers to the compass rose, adjusted the course. Dish-washing machines ground in the galley; in the dining saloon, waiters set up for breakfast and speculated about tips to be received. And Stewardess Felicia Brown found the Old Respectables' missing sword.

She was not looking for it. She was doing her nightly chores. When she got her chores done, she would go below decks to the cabin she shared with Mrs. Palsey and Mrs. Fish and young Miss Pratt—a bit of a flibbertigibbet, Miss Pratt—and get the sleep she had earned. It would be fine to get her feet up. Her feet were killing her. It was a pity some of these people with nothing to do but stuff themselves and sit in the sun, couldn't turn down their own beds.

Mrs. Brown knocked on the door of Cabin 84, forward on the starboard side of A Deck and, being unanswered, opened the door and went in and turned down the beds. One of them had been napped on, and had to be smoothed out. You'd think, what with deck chairs, they'd manage to stay off the beds in the daytime. For any purpose, she thought, and mildly dusted the dressing table, on which powder had been spilled. She held a bottle of perfume to her nose and shook her head and put it down again.

She went aft to Cabin 86 and knocked, and waited, and went in and turned down the beds. Most nights, it went on like this, never meeting anybody to pass the time of day with. Like as not, most of them thought the beds turned themselves down; from the tips one got,

one'd think that. The breakfasts in were different.
Then you could make yourself felt. This way—

She went out of Cabin 86, and knocked on the door
of Cabin 88. Again there was no answer. She pushed
on the door and there was resistance. One of them had
left a valise or something in the way, which was like
some of them. She pushed harder and the door partially opened, and she began to wedge herself through
the opening. She got far enough to see—far enough to
find the sword.

The sword was in J. Orville Marsh, who lay on his
back on the floor. He had bled on the carpet. The
sword was not all the way in, but far enough. It didn't
take a doctor to know it was far enough. The amount
of blood told that.

Mrs. Brown wanted to scream. She also wanted to
be sick. But it was not her place to scream, or to be
sick. Leave that sort of thing to "them." She went, as
fast as heavy old legs would carry her, to authority.
Authority was not the highest—it was an assistant
purser. It served. . . .

It was a little after eleven. Dorian Weigand was
propped up in bed, looking extremely lovely, reading—but not as if hopelessly engrossed. There was a
telephone in the room, Bill Weigand thought, hanging
his white dinner jacket in a closet, reaching to loosen
his black tie. There was a telephone, but this time it
would not ring, as so often it rang. The policeman's life
is an interrupted one, but not tonight—not here, far
from land, in the snugness of this cabin, on this gently
rocking ship. There would be no sudden calls—no
sudden canceling of leave. If they wanted him back,
tonight, they would have to come after him. By heli-
copter. Half of New York could kill the other half, and
Captain William Weigand, Homicide, Manhattan

West, would help worry about it another time. In, say, a week. Now—

Now somebody knocked at the cabin door. The knocking was not loud, but it was insistent. Pam or Jerry, presumably, with some sudden idea. Not that it would be like either of them. But still—The most reliable people may relax on vacation, and give exaggerated value to sudden ideas. Like, even, joining together for a nightcap.

Bill Weigand went to the door and opened it, fixing on his face a smile as cordial as he could manage. The knocker was not a North. The knocker was Cholly, captain's steward. Cholly's face was, for it, a little pale. Cholly's white teeth tugged at his lower lip.

"Captain's compliments, sir," Cholly said. "He'd appreciate it if you could come to his quarters."

"Now?" Bill said.

"He'd appreciate it, sir," Cholly said. "He said to tell you it's urgent, sir."

Bill looked at him.

"Very urgent, sir," Cholly said. "The captain would very much appreciate it, sir."

Bill continued to look at the boy, who wasn't beamish at all at the moment.

"It's about the sword, sir," Cholly said. "The captain said I could tell you they've—they've found the sword."

"Right," Bill said. "Wait a minute."

He closed the door. He looked at Dorian.

"Damn," Dorian Weigand said, not loudly but with conviction.

"Right," Bill said. "But—there we are."

He leaned over the bed and kissed her.

"Oh," Dorian said. "I know it isn't your fault. Go find out about the sword. Nevertheless—damn."

Bill followed the steward along the corridor of A Deck; to the elevator and into it. When the elevator stopped, he went up a short flight of steel stairs, still following Cholly. Cholly knocked and Captain Peter Cunningham, RNR, opened the door at once.

"Oh," he said. "Glad you could make it. Appreciate your coming, Weigand." He led the way back into the cabin. He said, "Scotch?" Bill shook his head.

Captain Cunningham nodded. His long, intelligent face was not particularly expressive. He did not look worried. On the other hand, he looked by no means happy.

"As a matter of fact," Captain Cunningham said, "a rather sticky situation has come up." He considered this. "As a matter of fact," he said, "quite a sticky situation."

It was not often, Bill Weigand realized, that Captain Peter Cunningham, RNR, went, thus, into superlatives. All hell had, apparently, broken loose.

"Your boy," Bill said, "tells me the sword's been found."

"Quite," Captain Cunningham said, and told him where.

Bill listened.

"You don't," Captain Cunningham said, "seem greatly surprised."

"You send a steward for me, fairly late at night," Bill said. "He says the matter's urgent, and mentions the sword. In effect, I said, earlier, that the sword would concern me only if it was found in someone. I supposed it had been." He smiled, faintly. "In short," he said, "I'd already had my surprise."

"Not a pleasant one," Cunningham said. "And—I realize it's none of your concern. Only—well, there's this."

This was a message on a radiogram form. It was signed "Follonby." It read:

"Take appropriate measures but urge discretion to avoid disturbing passengers. Weigand on your list is police officer experienced such matters and might be asked assist at your discretion."

"Follonby's the managing director," Cunningham said. "Great man for discretion. See his point, though. No use stirring up—" He stopped with a shrug. "What it comes to," he said. "Will you lend a hand? Hate to ask you, but there it is. I can promise you the company'll be generous."

"No," Bill said. "Oh—yes, I'll lend a hand. But New York City hires me. And—I don't like murder. Particularly of—" He paused. "In a way," he said, "Marsh was on our side. We don't like things to happen to people on our side. You've moved the body?"

They had not. An assistant purser was standing by, as unobtrusively as possible, to see that no one did.

"For one thing," Captain Cunningham said, "people'll be up and about for hours. Have to take him through passageways, y'know. On the other hand—well, the room's not air-conditioned. We're heading south. Have to—er—refrigerate in the course of time."

"Right," Bill said. "You've seen it?"

"Yes," Cunningham said. "I've seen it. With the doctor. That gold hilt sticking up in the air—doesn't seem right, somehow. Shell splinter—that sort of thing makes some kind of sense. But this—What did they want with a sword?"

They had wanted it, Bill told him, to carry in a parade.

"Silly sort of business," Captain Cunningham said. "Shall we get along?"

They got along. They went down in the elevator to A Deck and Bill followed the captain along the corridor to Cabin 88. The movement of the ship was somewhat more apparent than it had been—at least to Bill Weigand. From Captain Cunningham's balanced progress down the corridor, one would never have known it. "Swell's from the one that sheered off," Captain Cunningham said, over his shoulder, referring to a hurricane which, some days before, had gone elsewhere, after giving the Eastern seaboard a week-long fright. "Be out of it tomorrow."

They had to make themselves thin to get through the partially openable door of Cabin 88. Fortunately, this was not difficult for either of them. Inside a young man in uniform turned from a porthole, out of which he had been looking. He did not look as if he felt particularly well. "Captain Weigand, Forbes," Cunningham said. "You can shove off, now."

"Yes sir," the assistant purser said. He went carefully, as distantly as space allowed, around what was on the floor, and made himself thin going out of the door. Weigand was crouched beside the body.

J. Orville Marsh lay on his back, in a position which seemed incongruously comfortable. The sword stuck straight up from his chest, most of it above his body but enough—oh, quite enough—in it. With the motion of the ship the gilded hilt moved slowly back and forth, seeming to bow to them; seeming to perform a slow, macabre dance.

"Ribs holding it," Weigand said. "Through the heart, apparently."

"Dr. Wilson said that," the captain told him. "Between ribs, into the heart. A lucky thrust, from one point of view. Shall we have the doctor in?''

They needn't, at the moment, Bill thought. Presumably the doctor had told Captain Cunningham what there was to tell.

The doctor had. One thrust of the thin, sharp steel into the chest of J. Orville Marsh, Marsh dying of it within, at the outside, a minute or so. A stewardess had found the body between nine thirty and nine forty-five. The doctor had seen it about fifteen minutes later—say at ten o'clock. Marsh had not been longer than an hour dead; perhaps less.

Bill nodded and stood up. He looked at the door, down at the body. The ship's captain waited.

"Probably," Bill said, "someone knocked. He opened the door. Somebody stood there with the sword ready. Stabbed him while he was standing there, before he had a chance to move. And closed the door. Or, falling backward, Marsh's feet hit the door and pushed it closed. Is there a ship's photographer?''

"Well," Cunningham says, "there's a gal takes pictures. Of people in the café, y'know. But—"

Bill waited.

"Hate to call her just now," Cunningham said. "Be a little obvious, wouldn't it? As a matter of fact, take pictures myself now and then. Amateur stuff. Wife and kiddies. That sort of silly business. Still—"

"Flashlight?" Bill asked him.

"Matter of fact," the captain said, "yes. Have a shot at it, if you like."

"Right," Bill said.

Cunningham used the telephone. Cholly, very quickly, arrived with camera, rigged for flashlight. It was, Bill saw, a very good camera. Photographing the remains of J. Orville Marsh, the captain used it expertly. After he had, as Bill directed, shot from half a dozen angles, he looked at Bill enquiringly. Bill thought they had what they wanted.

Bill twisted a handkerchief into a short rope, looped it through the sword hilt and pulled. The sword clung for a moment; came out with a faint, unpleasant sound. Marsh had been deep chested. Some inches of the sword were bloody. Blood dripped from the tip of the sword. The rest of the blade was bright in the ceiling light; it looked sharp. It had, obviously, been sharp enough. Pam, Bill remembered, had called it a toy sword. It had proved a venomous toy.

"Took a bit of doing?" Cunningham said. "To make the thrust, I mean?"

"Some," Bill told him. "But the point's sharp—and missed bone."

He looked at the dangling sword. The pommel was ridged for sure gripping. The gilding of the hilt was fretted with design. They would look for prints—somehow—and find blurs. Too many blurs, made by too many Old Respectables. Bill knotted the handkerchief and hung the sword by it from a closet hook. It had stopped dripping.

As he turned back, the movement of the ship caught him unawares. He did not precisely stagger, but he swayed toward Captain Cunningham, who did not sway at all.

"Won't be in it long," Captain Cunningham assured him. Bill Weigand's eyes had narrowed slightly, and the captain stopped and waited.

"If I'd happened to have a sword pointing at you, I might have run you through," Bill said. "A—what? Fifty-fifty chance?"

Captain Cunningham moved his head slowly up and down. "About that," he said.

He waited.

"It may have been that way," Bill said. "But, we're a long way from knowing. From knowing anything, except the obvious." He leaned down and looked under one of the beds—Marsh, not sparing of expense, had booked a double cabin. There were two large suitcases under the bed. There was a dispatch case.

"You'll want to go through these things," Captain Cunningham said, and Bill nodded. He would also want to see the doctor, the stewardess who had found the body. To, he explained, keep things neat. But—

He looked at the body. The cabin was reasonably large, but not large enough for what it contained.

"Rather in the way, isn't he?" Captain Cunningham said. "But I'd like to wait—oh, say a couple of hours? Longer, if possible. As a matter of—" He paused. "Discretion," he said. "No use—"

He was interrupted. Someone was knocking at the cabin door. Cunningham started around the body toward the door, but Bill touched his arm. He pointed. He indicated. They pulled Marsh's body far enough into the cabin so the door would open. The knocking was repeated. This time, Bill nodded. Captain Cunningham opened the door. He said, "Good Evening?" to J. R. Folsom. Folsom was still in uniform. He said, "Oh!" in a surprised tone. He said, "What goes—" He looked into the room. He said, *"My God!"*

"Quite," Captain Cunningham said. He turned and looked at Bill Weigand.

"Right," Bill said. "What brings you here, Mr. Folsom?"

Respected Captain Folsom, although symbolically dressed for the violence of battle, stood in the doorway with his mouth open—and his eyes wide, and a certain pastiness of complexion. He pointed.

"He—" he said, and stopped to swallow. "Something's happened to him?" He looked at the color of the carpet, which had once been a pleasant gray. "My God!" he said.

"He's dead," Bill said. "That's where the sword was, Mr. Folsom." He moved to the closet, and unhooked the sword, and let it dangle from the handkerchief. "Did you come for it?"

Folsom made a slight retching sound, and visibly took a deep breath, and conquered it.

"Going to meet him in the bar," Folsom said. "Have a nightcap. He didn't show so I—what do you mean, did I come for it? What the hell right've you got—"

"Captain Weigand is trying to find out what happened," Cunningham said. "At my request, Mr. Folsom. With my authority."

"All the same—" Folsom said, and stopped again.

"You were going to meet Mr. Marsh for a drink," Bill said. "He didn't show up and you came to find him?"

Folsom said, "Yeh."

"There's a telephone in the smoking lounge," Bill said. "All you had to do was to ask to be connected with Mr. Marsh's room." He regarded Folsom. "Saved yourself a walk," he said.

"Well," Folsom said. "I didn't think of it. That's all. I didn't think of it. You always think of everything?"

He was aggrieved. It appeared his feelings were hurt.

"You trying to make me the goat?" Folsom asked, and now he was more aggrieved than ever. "Just because somebody stole our sword? If I killed him, what would I be coming back for?" This thought brightened him. "Tell me that," he said, speaking with something approaching triumph.

"All right," Bill said. "I did tell you—to get the sword."

"What did I knock for?" Folsom said. "Look—you say I killed him. So I know he's dead, don't I? So why do I knock? Dead people don't open doors."

Cunningham looked at Bill Weigand. He raised his eyebrows.

"All right," Bill said. "I didn't say you killed him. Come on in. And—tell us more about the sword."

Unhappily, Respected Captain J. R. Folsom came in.

4

The sword had last been worn by an officer of the day—Sergeant Walter D. Riggs, real estate—on the tour of duty which had ended at midnight, a little less than twenty-four hours earlier. Between midnight and eight in the morning, the Ancient and Respectable Riflemen dispensed with sentry. (It appeared, although it was not specifically said, that the officer of the day was a species of perambulating sergeant-at-arms, intended to help Ancient and Respectable Riflemen keep themselves under control.) J. R. Folsom was the first to admit that the lack of night patrol was to be lamented.

"To be frank with you," Folsom said, with the air of one who puts cards on a table, "the boys just won't do it. Not at night. Hard enough to keep them at it—" He stopped.

In any case, Sergeant Riggs had put the sword in one of the two rifle boxes at midnight—perhaps a little before midnight. He had gone, then, to the smoking saloon, leaving Adjutant Hammond Jones—Jones Bros. Buick Corp.—to lock up.

"Why?" Bill asked. "Why didn't Riggs lock up?"

"Jonesy's got the key," Folsom said, in some surprise. "Adjutant's responsibility."

"Go ahead," Bill told him.

The rifle boxes were stored forward and inboard on the promenade deck, rather in the way of the athletic doing their eight circuits to the mile. The boxes were there so that, when it came time to parade, the rifles could be got at. Once case had been left locked; the other, for the benefit of the sword, was locked only during the night. But the night before, "Jonesy just plain forgot it," Folsom told them. "What with one thing and another. Not that Jonesy's what you'd call a drinking man."

Sometime between midnight and morning, the sword had disappeared from the case. Sergeant O'Brien—James J. O'Brien, flooring—had gone for it at eight, or maybe a little after. It was not there.

"Are you all officers?" Weigand asked. "Or noncoms?"

"Well," Folsom said, "I wouldn't go that far. But frankly, mostly. Way we work it, new members are privates for six months. Indoctrination. After that—"

"Right," Bill said. "Sergeant O'Brien told you, I suppose?"

"Woke me up," Folsom said, with some retrospective bitterness. "Told him to follow the chain. Chain of command. Told him to go wake up Adjutant Jones. Have Jones report to me. Chain of command, like I said. Anyway, Jonesy was the man supposed to lock up."

"What did you do to find it?" Bill said.

They had asked around. All the Old Respectables had denied any knowledge of the sword.

"And," Bill said, "you figured somebody had taken

it out, all the same? Hidden it—as—as a joke of some sort?"

"Well," Folsom said, "some of them didn't like to wear it. Like I said, because it banged into things. Maybe, come down to it, some of the boys thought it was a little silly." Folsom stopped. "That's only what I thought then," he said. "Way it is now—"

"The way it is now," Bill said, "you'd rather think it wasn't one of the riflemen?"

"Way it is now," Folsom said, "I think anybody on the boat could have got it. All our boys are good one hundred per cent Americans."

Captain Peter Cunningham blinked.

"You mean," he asked, politely, "that Americans— one hundred per cent Americans, that is—do not kill people?"

"Oh," Folsom said. "See what you mean, captain. Not with swords, see what *I* mean?"

Captain Cunningham looked as if he were about to say he didn't.

"Why," Bill Weigand said, "was the sword kept sharp, Mr. Folsom? Since I assume it was a ceremonial sword?"

Folsom did not answer immediately. Then he said, "Well—" and paused again.

"Well," Folsom said, "I guess you'd say on account of Junior." He looked from Weigand to Captain Cunningham, as if about to ask them whether they knew what he meant; he appeared to assume they did not.

"Well," he said, "Junior's my son. We call him Junior. Mighty fine young—" He began to reach into his tunic. "Got a picture here some—"

"Never mind," Bill said. "I'm sure he is. The sword was sharpened up for Junior?"

Folsom nodded.

"Why?" Bill asked him, with as much restraint as he could manage.

"To cut the cake," Folsom said. "What did you think I meant?"

"I," Bill said, "had no idea at all. A wedding cake?"

"Sure," Folsom said. "Junior got married last June. Mighty fine young lady he—" He looked at Weigand. "O.K.," he said. "Junior got married. But the draft's caught up with him. They decided to get married first. His mother didn't approve but—there you are. So, as he was going into the Army, I thought, why the hell not? Only, when I looked at it, the sword looked pretty dull and—well, not shined up right. So I sent it to these people and they fixed it up and put an edge on it. That's all there was to that."

Involuntarily, he looked at the sword—the sword dangling in sight, which had, in its last use but one, sliced through a wedding cake. He looked away again.

"The only reason you came here," Bill said, "was to find out why Mr. Marsh hadn't showed up for a drink at the bar?"

"Yeh," Folsom said, and spoke quickly. "That's all I came for. And—I wish to hell I hadn't."

"All right," Bill said. "Go along and have your drink, Mr. Folsom. And—" His glance passed it to Captain Cunningham.

"I'd appreciate it," Captain Cunningham said, "if you'd say as little about this as possible, Mr. Folsom. As a matter of fact—if you'd say nothing about it at all." He paused to smile. "No use having people get the wind up, is there?" he said. "This sort of thing—" He paused again. "Leave a taste in the mouth, wouldn't it?" he said.

Folsom saw what he meant. After a final quick

glance at what was on the floor, Folsom got out of Cabin 88. Cunningham raised his eyebrows at Bill Weigand.

"I don't know," Bill said. "He could have come for that. Newfound pal. He's had a few. Perhaps enough to make old friends out of strangers. But—what was the matter with the telephone?"

Cunningham shook his head.

"On the other hand," he said, "man's got a point. If he killed Marsh, why come back?"

Weigand shrugged. He indicated the telephone between the two beds. He asked whether, on that, he could get ship-to-shore. He could. Weigand edged around the body, but the captain was nearer and picked up the telephone. He waited briefly. "Captain here," he said. "A shore call coming. I'd like you to expedite." Then he handed the telephone to Weigand. Weigand wanted the offices of Homicide, Manhattan West, in West Twentieth Street. He gave the number. He said, "Thanks," and hung up the telephone. He said, "How many passengers have you aboard, captain?" and groaned slightly when he was told there were a hundred and forty or thereabouts. Told that there were as many more in the crew—that there were close to three hundred men and women and children aboard the *Carib Queen*—he groaned audibly.

It was several minutes later that the telephone rang. Bill was pulling the second of two large suitcases from under one of the beds. He put it on the bed with its mate, and with a flat attaché case. He answered the telephone and talked, across miles of water which shone under a three-quarters' moon, to Sergeant Stein in a small, and somewhat dingy, office in Tenth Precinct station house in West Twentieth Street, Manhattan. He wanted what could be found out about one J. Orville Marsh, licensed private investigator, deceased; one J. R. Folsom, manufacturer of paper boxes in Worcester, Mass.; one Mrs. Olivia Macklin, home address not given except as New York City, and one Hilda Macklin, her daughter; one Oscar Peterson, miller, from Minnesota, and his wife; one Walter D. Riggs, real estate, also of Worcester, and one Hammond Jones, Buick dealer, of the same city and—He said to wait a minute.

"The others at your table, captain?" Bill said. "Young couple; elderly couple."

The captain looked puzzled; he gave names. "Mr. and Mrs. Carl Buckley, some place in Kansas. Mr. and Mrs. Aaron Furstenberg, Central Park West," Bill told Sergeant Stein, over static. "And—get hold of the passenger list. Have the identification boys go over it. See if any of our favorite names show up. Right?"

"O.K., captain," Stein said. "Having a nice trip?"

"Wonderful," Bill said. "Entirely wonderful, sergeant. Man with a sword in him. Mullins' new baby showed up?"

"Boy," Stein said. "Eight pounds six ounces. What you want'll take time."

Bill Weigand knew it would. As things cropped up, if things did crop up, information could be telephoned along. It would be useful if it could also be air-mailed to Havana. He hung up.

"Folsom I understand," Captain Cunningham said. "And Jones—Adjutant Jones—and Riggs. Buy why the Petersons, Mrs. Macklin and the Buckleys and Furstenbergs? Nice young couple, the Buckleys. Interesting accent. Why?"

"Mrs. Macklin makes herself felt," Bill said. "As

for the others—we have to start some place. Also, they've met Marsh." He smiled at Cunningham's expression. "Oh," he said, "I know it's tenuous. I know we'll be wasting time. But—three fourths of all the motions we go through are wasted motions." He looked at the ship's captain, used to more orderly procedures. Captain Cunningham merely looked interested. "Before we can make a fix," Bill said. "That's the word, isn't it?"

"Oh," Cunningham said. "Quite, Weigand."

Bill got on with it. He got on first, with a suitcase which, lifted, had felt empty. It was empty. He went to the other suitcase, which had not felt empty. It was not. Marsh had been using it as a hamper for soiled clothes. He had made several changes. Either he was a man of very scrupulous cleanliness, or he had brought soiled clothing aboard. It might be, Weigand thought, that he had spent a few nights in a hotel before embarking. He rummaged in the clothing. He found a .38 caliber, police positive, revolver. He took it out. It was loaded.

"I thought," Cunningham said, "you told me that Marsh didn't carry a gun?"

Bill had. He admitted he had. It appeared he had been wrong. He emptied the clothing in the case onto the bed and further examined the case. He found nothing; he tossed the clothing back in. He turned to the attaché case—a smooth, rectangular box of leather. It was locked. Cunningham watched him.

"Here," Cunningham said, "let me have a go at it, what?"

He produced a heavy knife, and opened a heavy blade. He prized at the lock. He broke the blade of the knife.

"Bad steel," Cunningham said. He opened another blade and prized again, more carefully. His hands were deft; when it became necessary, they were strong. The brass tongue of the lock snapped up. "There we are," Captain Cunningham said, pleased.

The shallow case was only partly filled. One by one, Bill Weigand took objects from it.

He took a square brown envelope and opened it and four glossy photographs slid out. They were photographs of jewelry—of a wide bracelet, heavily jeweled; of a ring, with a single large setting—again probably a diamond; of two necklaces, presumably of pearls. All these pretty things had been photographed against black cloth; Bill presumed, black velvet. He held the photographs out to the captain, who looked at them. The captain said they looked like money—like a great deal of money.

Bill agreed to that, adding that one couldn't tell. The diamonds might be glass, the pearls graduated beads.

"Silly to photograph them if they were," Cunningham said, reasonably. Bill agreed to that, and went on.

There was a photograph of a heavy, elderly woman with white hair. She wore a dark dress. Her eyes and her face seemed sad, and her face drooped sadly. Bill showed this to the captain, and Cunningham shook his head.

"Nor I," Bill said, and turned the photograph over, and found nothing written on the back of it.

Bill opened a black notebook and a letter fell out of it. There was no envelope. There was the discreet letterhead of The Clover Club. There was nothing to say where The Clover Club might be. The letter was dated October 3. It was addressed to "Dear Mr. Marsh." It read:

"Nothing has come up to change the situation, so this will confirm our verbal agreement, terms and all. But for God's sake, use kid gloves."

The note was signed. It was signed in a swirl of circling lines, which conveyed precisely nothing.

"It looks," Captain Cunningham said, "as if Marsh weren't so retired as he said." He studied the signature. "Pity," he said, "that people never learn to write their names."

It was. Bill agreed to that. It was a great pity. He leafed the notebook, slowly at first, then more quickly. He handed it to Captain Cunningham, who looked, too, at several pages; who shook his head over them.

It might be—it might well be—that here, on these pages, was all they needed to know. J. Orville Marsh, private investigator—who still, it might be assumed, was investigating when he died—had kept notes. He had cannily kept them in shorthand.

It was doubly unfortunate that the shorthand method was not one of those commonly in use. A detective has a smattering of much knowledge. Bill Weigand had, of shorthand, enough to tell him this.

It is difficult to empty the pockets of a heavy man who lies, fully clothed and fully dead, in a cramped space. It can be managed; two men can manage it, but it is not easy, particularly when the man lies in blood. Weigand and Captain Peter Cunningham did it. Neither enjoyed it, but they got it done. Afterward they washed their hands. Then they looked at what they had.

They had keys, in a case. They had two clean handkerchiefs, one from the breast pocket of a dinner jacket which had been white, and was no longer white. They had a half-empty package of Camels, and a Zippo lighter and a dollar and thirty-seven cents in small

change. They had a Cyma automatic wrist watch on a
leather strap, and a pair of glasses in a leather case.
Weigand held the glasses up to the light and moved
them back and forth. He decided Marsh had been far-
sighted, and needed corrective lenses when he read.
They had a folder of American Express checks—four
hundred and fifty dollars, in denominations of fifty,
one torn out on the perforation. And they had J.
Orville Marsh's billfold, initialed "J.O.M." in gold
leaf.

The billfold contained two hundred and thirteen
dollars in bills. It contained an identification card,
showing that Marsh had been duly licensed as a private investigator by the New York Police Department.
It contained a pistol permit, allowing Marsh the possession of a .38 police positive, of recorded serial
number. It contained a permit to operate a motor
vehicle and passenger vehicle registration for a 1954
Chevrolet sedan. An insurance service card showed
that the car was insured with Aetna. A credit card
proved that Marsh had, at least in 1952, been autho-
rized to charge what he liked at the Buckminster Hotel
in West Forty-third Street. For good measure, Marsh
had joined the Diners' Club.

And in the billfold there was a check for five hundred dollars, made out to J. Orville Marsh, drawn on a
Worcester, Massachusetts, bank—and signed with the
same indecipherable twist of circling lines which was
at the bottom of the letter which confirmed a "verbal"
agreement.

And at that, Bill Weigand swore softly, in helpless-
ness and exasperation. Some hundreds of miles away,
across much water and parts of three states, there
were people—any number of people, from operators

of bookkeeping machines to bank presidents—who could glance at this meaningless scrawl and say, "of course, Mr. Smith. Or Mr. Brown. Or Mr. Ezekial Jerome Winterbottom, the Third." And then a policeman, tactfully, could ask Mr. Smith-Brown-Winterbottom what he had agreed on "verbally" with J. Orville Marsh, and afterward confirmed both by letter and by check. And that would be that, for what it might be worth.

It might have nothing to do with the death of Mr. Marsh, upon whom somebody had fallen with a sword. (Perhaps, Bill thought, more or less literally.) It might have everything to do. The exasperating thing was that they had no means of finding out. If the *Carib Queen* were equipped for the dispatch of radio photographs— but that was absurd. He nevertheless mentioned it to Captain Peter Cunningham. It was absurd. The *Carib Queen* was equipped for many things, some rather more complex than picture transmission. She could look through darkness, farther than the eye could reach. Electronically, when near the coast—as she was now—the *Carib Queen* could tell herself precisely where she was. But she could not dispatch the convoluted signature on note and check to Worcester, Massachusetts, where it would mean something.

"Folsom's merry men come from Worcester," Cunningham said, and looked at Bill Weigand and said, "Sorry, old man. Realize you know that."

"Right," Bill said. He put the contents of Marsh's pockets into the attaché case. "It can be coincidence, of course." He picked up the confirming note and gazed at it again. He handed it to Cunningham, who gazed at it, too—who held it under a lamp on the dressing table and gazed at it long, who handed it back and shook his head. "Could be damn' near anything," Cunningham said.

Bill used the telephone again. There was, at any rate, that. He added a few points for Sergeant Stein, who had got things moving from a desk, its edges scarred with cigarette burns, in West Twentieth Street. Tomorrow—which unfortunately would be Sunday, when information is hard to come by—they might find out whether there was a Clover Club in Worcester, Massachusetts, and whether one of its members had a peculiarly meaningless signature. The following day, they might enquire, to the same effect, of the Bay State-Farmer's Trust in Worcester.

He didn't, Stein said, without reproach, give them much to go on. A good many men hid their identity in their signatures. Bill realized that. He said, "It's a sort of circular squiggle," and listened to Stein and smiled, and said he realized it didn't, but that there it was.

"Marsh lived at the Buckminster," Stein said. "Had for years. Highly valued guest and all that sort of thing. The boys are going through his room. It'll be slow going about the rest. It's the middle of the night, here. In fact, it's Sunday, here."

"It is here, too," Bill told him. "Unless you get something hot—and you won't—call me in the morning."

"O.K.," Stein said. "I'll get on with it."

Bill could see him, in the small, familiar, distant room, with a cigarette smouldering on the edge of the desk, reaching out for a telephone. He could see "the boys" going through Marsh's room; checking out on the passenger list—if they had got hold of it, and they would have got hold of it. It was consolation, of sorts. It would have been more consolation to have Sergeant

Aloysius Mullins aboard the *Carib Queen*. Bill picked up the attaché case and, since it no longer had a lock, put it under an arm.

"There's nothing more to be done tonight," Bill said, and Cunningham looked, momentarily, as if he had been expecting a rabbit from a hat, and was let down at seeing none. But he said, "Right you are," and then, "anything I can do to help." He looked at Marsh. "Aside," he said, "from the matter of refrigeration."

"I don't—" Bill said, and stopped. "It might," he said, "be an idea to keep somebody in here after you've removed the body." Cunningham raised eyebrows. "On the chance," Bill said, "that somebody might want to tidy up."

Cunningham said, "Folsom? You think he'd—"

Bill only shrugged. He started for the door, and stopped.

"The Norths," he said, "have somehow—I've not always known quite how—been involved in several cases with me. Been—" He paused for the word. He chose "helpful," which was decidedly a compromise.

"Whatever you say, of course," Captain Cunningham said. "I'd rather hoped—"

Bill Weigand realized what the captain had rather hoped. But he shook his head.

"They'll probably help," he said. "In—one way or another. And they'll find out anyway. Mrs. North especially." He opened the door and started through it. "She always does," he added over his shoulder, and left Captain Peter Cunningham with the corpse which cumbered his bright, gay ship. And with a bloody sword to lock up somewhere—somewhere out of reach.

Since it was inevitable that Dorian be told what had happened, it was after two on Sunday morning when the Weigands slept. They were awakened a little after six, by the telephone on the stand between their beds.

"It's just the way it always is," Dorian said, sadly, as she watched her husband dress. "Damn," Dorian Weigand added.

5

But he was a baby, Pam North said. "Just a *baby!*" she said, and spoke hotly. "What was he thinking of?"

It was a little after ten o'clock on Sunday morning. They were in the Norths' cabin, Dorian curled on one made-up bed; Pam leaning forward, sitting tailor-fashion in slacks, on the other. Jerry sat in a chair and Bill Weigand stood by one of the portholes, now and then looking out to where, beyond the moving shadow of the ship, the early sun sparkled on the water. The water was very blue to the westward, where the Gulf Stream flowed toward the north.

Charles Pinkham was twenty, Bill said. He was almost twenty-one. Grant he looked younger—had the round pink face of youth, and was called "Cholly," an appellation calculated to minimize maturity. Nevertheless, he was almost old enough to vote. He weighed better than a hundred and fifty; behind his beamish expression and steward's gentle manners, he might well be tough. Men younger than he had sheltered themselves in fox-holes—had died in them.

As for what Captain Peter Cunningham had been

thinking of, he had been thinking of keeping what rein he could on rumor. Cholly already knew where the sword had been found; he had acted as messenger. He was trustworthy, as young men went—young men with a great secret.

"I asked him to have somebody stay there," Bill said. "He picked young Pinkham. I would have done the same, probably."

"And the boy," Pam said, "the baby, is dying of it."

She would not, for the moment, be argued with. Jerry North looked at Bill and shrugged, just perceptibly. The shrug was meant to reassure. "It's no good to humor me," Pam said, darkly. "I think what I think. He had officers take the body away. Why not have one of them stay?"

"He's not dying of it," Bill said. "At least—the doctor hopes he isn't. The officers have fixed duties, I suppose. He's got a concussion, and perhaps a fracture. The immediate point is—he's unconscious."

"I suppose," Pam said, "there's no use crying over broken heads? All he amounts to is a witness who can't talk? Is that it?" She was not answered. "Oh, all right," Pam North said. "Now that we're official, we have to take the official stand."

They were, at any rate, more official than they had ever been before. Before, officialdom—in the choleric person of Deputy Chief Inspector Artemus O'Malley—had snorted at the mere mention of their names. Now, insofar as Bill Weigand was official—deriving from the ship's captain, who derived from British maritime law—they were too, at only one remove. They had even been asked; such evidence as there was was spread before them.

The evidence was, to put it conservatively, incomplete. It was especially incomplete on the slugging, probably with a blackjack, of young Charles Pinkham, captain's steward, in the cabin formerly occupied by J. Orville Marsh.

Cholly—no longer beamish as he lay in a bed in what Captain Cunningham referred to as sick bay, but still likely to recover—had been slugged sometime between two and six in the morning. That much was clear. At two, junior officers of the ship, equipped with a stretcher, had taken Marsh's body out of the cabin and, quietly, down passageways to a place of refrigeration. They had left Cholly in the room, advising him to keep his wits about him.

That he evidently had failed to do. He was found at six by an assistant purser. Young Pinkham was lying on the floor, much as Marsh had lain on the floor. But Pinkham was breathing heavily and the carpet was no more bloodied than it had been.

He had been hit on the side of the head, above the right ear. The skin had not been broken, which suggested a blackjack expertly used. (Or something with sand in it.) How long he had been unconscious when he was found, the ship's surgeon could not say. Possibly, several hours. He was dressed, except for his white jacket. One of the beds had been lain on; probably it had been slept on. Pinkham had been told to keep the cabin dark; he had been up since six the morning before. He had not been warned that there was any real likelihood of intrusion; he had realized he was there on an off-chance.

The cabin had been searched and there had been no effort to hide that fact. Marsh's clothing had been taken off hangers and gone through, and tossed aside. Drawers had been dumped, and their contents tossed about.

Since they had no way of knowing what had been

sought, they had none of knowing whether it had been found. They could hope not—they could hope they had it here. Bill indicated Marsh's belongings, from attaché case and pockets, which were on the bed in front of Pam. But Bill had not made a careful search the night before. He had planned on a careful search today, and the guarding of the stateroom overnight.

"Whatever is worth doing at all is worth doing at once," Pam said, heaping the last coals of her resentment on Bill Weigand's head. "But you couldn't know," she added, scraping them off again. "I'm just hindsighting."

"Of course," Dorian said, "it may not have been there at all. There may not actually have been anything. Somebody may merely have been afraid there was."

They had their alternatives—what was sought existed, shapeless, only in someone's fears; it had been overlooked by Bill Weigand and found by someone else; it was among the things on the foot of the bed, just beyond Pam North's toes. If it remained in the stateroom, it was unrecognizable. Bill's examination, if late, had finally been complete. If the secret was in Marsh's notebook, it was likely to remain there, at least for a time.

Bill had sought out the ship's stenographer, carrying the book. She had looked at it and—quite literally, as it happened—thrown up her hand. "All I know," the stenographer said—she had quick, pretty hands, with pointed fingers—"all I know, it isn't Gregg. Anyway, not any Gregg *I* ever saw. And I've seen some scrawls."

Conceivably, it might be Pitman, or some modification of Pitman. She wouldn't know about that. Most probably, it was no standard system—many attempts had been made to improve on the standard systems, and few had lasted. But, here and there, a variant was remembered by someone, and used by someone. Perhaps whoever wrote in the notebook—and she wasn't asking who, or being told—had used such a variant, more for the purposes of secrecy than for speed. If meant to be secret, it was, from her.

So that, for the time being, was that. Much could be found on the *Carib Queen,* but there was, understandably, a dearth of cryptographers. In New York, it would be easy enough to get Marsh's notes deciphered—unless, of course, they were in a private code. In that event, it might take time. But, thus cut off—cut off until Havana—there did not seem to be anything to do about the notebook.

They were left with a .38 revolver, photographs of an elderly woman and of articles of jewelry; a note and a check, sharing a signature which was itself a cryptogram, and the contents of Marsh's wallet and of his pockets. They had his eyeglasses and his wrist watch; they had several hundred dollars of his money.

Dorian and Pam and Jerry North had looked at these things, and shaken their heads over them. They looked at them again.

What they had to do, Pam pointed out, was to put two and two together. "It's supposed to be very easy," she said. "Like rolling off a log." She paused. "I've never really understood that one," Pam said. "What's so easy about rolling off a log?"

"Because they're round," Jerry told her, and was looked at doubtfully.

"Anyway," Pam said, letting it go. "Anyway—"

She considered, carefully, the photographed jewelry. "Are they real?" she asked, after scrutiny. "Because," she added, "I've had almost no experience with jewelry." She then, briefly, scrutinized Jerry North, who merely grinned at her. Bill Weigand turned from his thoughtful study of the blueness of the sea. He said that they had no way of telling that; that if they had the objects themselves—the bracelet, the ring, the two necklaces—they would still need an expert. Meanwhile, if it helped, they might assume them real, since there would be little point in the careful photography of rhinestones, of synthetic pearls.

"Put jewelry together," Pam said, "you get jewel thefts, of course. Then put this sad old lady with them and what do you get?"

They waited.

"Private detectives recover jewels," Pam said, and looked toward Bill Weigand, who nodded his head and, to the nod, added, "Sometimes."

"And capture the thieves?" Pam asked, and Bill said, "Not often. That isn't often the point." Pam waited. "Act as go-betweens, more frequently," Bill told her. "Between thief and insurance company— thief gets the reward, owner gets the jewelry, private investigator gets paid for his trouble. But I never heard Marsh was in that line of work."

"Nor," Dorian said, "do I see quite where it gets us."

She was, Pam said, merely looking for things to add. Jewelry, a sword, an elderly woman with sad eyes in a sad face, a man killed and a young man slugged, Ancient and Respectable Riflemen. "A little heap of things," Pam said, and Bill Weigand added to them. "A woman who says her stateroom was searched," he said. "A check and a letter. A notebook which we can't read. A—"

"Wait," Pam said. "The sad woman—" she indicated the photograph—"is a jewel thief. These are some of the jewels she's taken—part of a haul. Marsh was after her and—wait!"

The last came with a small yelp of triumph.

"That's how Mrs. Macklin comes in," Pam said. "That's plain, isn't it?"

It was not. It was not even plain, Jerry pointed out, that Mrs. Macklin came in at all. You couldn't, he said, start adding things to other things merely because— He discovered that the others were looking at him expectantly. He peered about his mind for an exit from a sentence which seemed to have closed around him. "Merely because they happen to be there," he said, and felt it feeble. Pam, at any rate, looked disappointed.

"That's very interesting, Jerry," Pam said, courteously. "You mean—we can't add—oh, apples and elephants? Merely because there *are* elephants?"

Jerry North ran the fingers of his right hand through his hair. It did not seem to him that that was precisely what he had meant.

"Of course," Dorian said, kindly, "he's quite right. We have to know which things to add. Or—we don't have to, but it would help."

"Well," Pam said, "somebody was searching Mrs. Macklin's room for jewelry. Start with that. This— jewel thief." She pointed to the photograph of the sad woman. "Of course," she said, "orchids make a great deal of difference."

Bill Weigand left the porthole. He sat down, rather carefully, in a chair. He said, "Orchids, Pam?"

"Oh," she said, "the general feel of orchids. And nice clothes and being on a cruise. Here—" here was again the photograph— "her face goes down. But with orchids, it might very well go up, which would make all the difference."

"You," Dorian said, "are thinking of the woman at the captain's table."

"Of course," Pam said. "With orchids. Make-up and everything. Couldn't she be?"

Dorian thought. She uncurled and reached for the photograph which Pam held out to her and curled again and looked at it. Finally, she said, "Mmmm."

"Exactly," Pam said. "That's just what I think. Mmmm."

Jerry looked at Bill Weigand.

"Your back's to them," Bill said. "The woman they're talking about at the captain's table is with her husband. A couple named Furstenberg. I can't say—" But he got up and got the photograph from his wife, and looked at it.

"All right," Pam said, "isn't it 'Mmmm'?"

The woman in the photograph and Mrs. Aaron Furstenberg were, probably, of about the same age—late sixties, at a guess. Both had white hair. Mrs. Furstenberg did not, by any means, look sad. But that, as Pam pointed out, might be the orchids, which was to say what the orchids stood for.

"A gang," Pam said. "Gang of two, anyway. Working the ships—probably some people who take cruises, even short cruises, have a lot of money. *And* jewelry. And Mr. Marsh was employed by—by—"

"An insurance company, possibly," Bill said. He looked at the photograph thoughtfully. There was nothing whatever to support Pam's theory. It was—it was merely one of those things which seemed to leap into her mind. It seemed unlikely that a jewel thief, even one on the verge of exposure, would turn murderer. But still—

"Mmmm," Bill Weigand said, and so paid tribute to

those things which leaped into Pamela North's mind. It was not that she was always right. It was more that she was seldom altogether wrong.

"The letter," Pam said, is from whoever it was—somebody at the insurance company—who hired Mr. Marsh. The check is, too. Not a regular company check because—" She paused. "Not let the left hand know what the right hand's doing," she said. "Marsh found out something—probably that they had been in Mrs. Macklin's stateroom. Then he tried to blackmail them, so they killed him. With Mr. Folsom's sword. Probably Mr.—what's the name again?—Furstenberg actually used the sword, because women don't. Daggers—yes. Swords—no. They're too long. And—"

"Pam," Jerry said. "Please, Pam."

"And then went back to the stateroom to see if there was anything which would give them away and—what, Jerry?"

"Whoa," Jerry said. "Just whoa, Pam. And—your bit's showing. The one in your teeth."

"All the same—" Pam said, and stopped. "Well," she said, "have you got a better idea?"

"Folsom and his merry men," Jerry said, gravely, "are really a gang of espionage agents. Working in a pack. Marsh was really F.B.I., playing a lone hand. They caught up with him. Marsh had the photographs of jewelry because he was thinking of buying his wife some and wanted to look at pictures. The sad woman is his wife. The—"

"Jerry!" Pam said. "She's much too old. And—"

"On the other hand," Dorian said, "Mrs. Macklin is a wealthy widow and people have moved in on her. The daughter isn't really her daughter—she's more of a wardress. The daughter and Marsh were working it together, gradually getting the money. Forcing her to sign checks and make over securities. Probably selling off her jewels. Mrs. Macklin, driven to desperation, turned on Mr. Marsh with a sword. Thinking that Marsh might have concealed evidence which would incriminate her, the daughter, Hilda, went to the stateroom and—"

"You," Pam said, "sound like a synopsis. Also, I like mine better. Bill?"

But Bill Weigand shook his head, slowly.

"I'm afraid," he said, "that I haven't any theory. But then, I haven't any facts. A man's dead and a younger man's been slugged. I—"

The telephone rang. Bill picked it up. He said, "Right," he listened. He said, "No. Put the rest in a radiogram, will you?" He listened and said, "Thanks." He replaced the receiver and looked, oddly, at Pam North.

"Sergeant Stein," he said. "There is a jewel thief aboard—at least, someone who was picked up last year for questioning and let go because the woman who'd lost the jewels wouldn't sign a complaint. Probably the insurance company reward racket. Going over the passenger list, one of the boys spotted it—a familiar name."

Pam's eyes widened slightly.

"Missis—" she began, but Bill was shaking his head.

"A man," he said. "Quite a young man—late twenties. A professional dancer. Name of Jules Barron."

"Oh," Pam said.

"Right," Bill said. "On the other hand—Aaron Furstenberg is a retired jeweler—manufacturing jeweler, and designer." He looked at Pam, still a little oddly.

"My goodness," Pam North said. "Things do go together, don't they?"

"The trouble is," Pam North told Jerry, "you've got stiffening of the moral fiber. It's very bad for people. At home, you don't think about walking all the time."

It was a little before noon and for an hour they had hardly thought of murder. On a lazy ship, moving serenely through bright waters, it is difficult to keep one's mind on things. In the bracing air of New York, spurred to endeavor by carbon monoxide, Pam would, she realized, have been up and about, not, as now, lethargic in a deck chair. If any murderer wanted to be caught, as long as the sun shone thus, he or she would have to come and ask for it. Pam had produced a theory and felt, uncharacteristically, exhausted by the effort. And now Jerry, who could usually be trusted as to mood, wanted her to walk the deck, eight to the mile. She would, she told him, as soon walk the plank. She mentioned his new ailment.

"At home," Pam said, "you sit at a desk and swivel. Anyway, after Labor Day."

"At home," Jerry said, "I do not eat large breakfasts, including kippers."

"Ugh," Pam said, with some difficulty.

"Nor large luncheons, including trifle," Jerry said. "Also, walking keeps me awake."

To find that Jerry, also, was in a lethargy from which even murder did not wholly arouse him was reasonably consoling. And, Pam further told herself, that had been the idea, really—a week of floating, an effortless week. Jerry had been looking tired, what with one author and another. Pam, stretched in the deck chair, oiled against the sun, wearing dark glasses to protect her eyes and enough bathing suit to satisfy minimum requirements, floated. After a while she would arouse herself—she would scrutinize Mrs. Furstenberg to see if, in droopier moments, she resembled the white-haired woman in the photograph—she would—

Someone sat down on the deck chair next to hers. Jerry had not, surely, already done his eight laps. Pam opened her eyes. It was not Jerry beside her. It was Mrs. Macklin. Pam turned her head and removed her glasses. She felt herself penetrated by Mrs. Macklin's gaze. It was like being transfixed by a double-barreled harpoon.

"Where is this detective?" Mrs. Macklin asked, her voice as sharp as her gaze, and then, before Pam could answer, "Don't tell me you don't know him. I saw you in the smoke room."

Pam started to speak.

"I've been looking for him all over," Mrs. Macklin said. "Upstairs *and* down. I want to hire him."

"Hire him?" Pam said. "Hire Captain Weigand?"

"Weigand?" Mrs. Macklin said. "What are you talking about, girl? What's he captain of? These toy soldiers?"

Pam sat up.

"Oh, you've got pretty legs," Mrs. Macklin said. "I'll give you that."

She was drunk again, Pam decided. It was early in the day for it, but Mrs. Macklin was drunk again. Only—she did not look drunk.

"Well?" Mrs. Macklin said.

"The New York City Police Department," Pam said.

"Oh," Mrs. Macklin said. "That one. You're talking about the wrong one. I don't want that one. The private one. Since nobody will do anything. You don't know where he is?"

"No," Pam said, and, when her conscience rustled faintly, told it that she didn't. Not precisely. Under refrigeration, of course. But where? "What did you want to hire him for, Mrs. Macklin?"

"You were there," Mrs. Macklin said. "Heard me tell the captain. Heard him promise he'd do something."

"Oh," Pam said, "about an intruder in your room? Didn't he?"

"Would I want to spend good money for a detective if he had?" Mrs. Macklin asked. "Tell me that."

Pam shook her head.

"I won't," Mrs. Macklin said, "be molested. Not any more. I'm not defenseless. They—"

Then, suddenly, she stopped and merely looked at Pam.

"I'm sure—" Pam began, and then Mrs. Macklin smiled. The smile was narrow in the tightness of her face, but it was friendly. Her voice, when she spoke, was quite a different voice.

"I shouldn't bother you with my troubles," she said. "I'm afraid I'm a little upset. Making a mountain out of a molehill. She says I am."

"Your daughter?" Pam said.

"Of course, dear," Olivia Macklin said, "my daughter. So patient with her flighty old mother."

From what Pam had seen of them together, what she saw now of Mrs. Macklin, Pam thought Hilda Macklin would have need of patience. Pam said, "Mmmm," which is a small sound that covers much.

"You don't know where the detective is, then?" Mrs. Macklin said. Pamela North shook her head. "When you see him, tell him I'm looking for him,"

Mrs. Macklin said, and nodded her head briskly. She wore a scarf over it—a pink scarf, her hair a fringe of red under it. "You'll do that?"

"Of course," Pam said.

Mrs. Macklin got up and went away. She moved resolutely. She did not walk as if she had been drinking.

After she had gone, Pam continued to sit erect on the deck chair for a moment. Then she dropped her robe behind her and walked the few paces on the gently moving deck to the swimming pool, and went into it. The water was cool, then it was tepid. Pam swam from end to end, and from end to end again, and stood at the shallow end and watched Hilda Macklin dive smoothly in at the deeper. She was certainly a different girl in a bathing suit, Pam thought, and watched with admiration. I do splash a lot, Pam thought. By comparison. She swam to the deep end of the pool and climbed the ladder, and looked back at Hilda, who was gliding. That was the only word for it.

Pam went to her chair, and her towel and robe. She wondered absently where the others were, and supposed Bill to be, in some fashion, at constabulary duty, and Dorian sketching and Jerry—Jerry had probably gone to their room to lie down. She decided to go and see and that it was, in any case, almost time to change for lunch. She went down the stairs to A Deck, and along the passageway to their stateroom, and found the door unlocked and went into it.

Jerry was not there. There was no one there.

Pam slid out of her bathing suit and regarded herself in the long mirror. From a distance, she thought, anyone might think I was still wearing the suit, what there is of it. When I get home, I'll have to get a sun lamp to even things out.

Carrying the wet bathing suit—what there was of it—Pam went across the stateroom toward the compact bath. The narrow door to the bath was closed. Pam opened it and at the same time flicked the switch, outside, which would send power through a fluorescent tube—make it first sputter, then flicker, then glow brightly. She would hang the—

The tube began to splutter. At that instant, hands came out of the small bath compartment. Pam was conscious of the hands as something moving—then as hands—then, while the light still flickered in the darkness, did not yet reveal who was hidden there, she was at the mercy of the hands. They whirled her around. She was thrust away by the hands, so that she staggered. Then she seemed to leave the floor as the hands, gripping her upper arms, hurled her across the stateroom.

Pam North sailed—could feel herself sailing. And she landed on one of the beds. She heard herself say, "*Uh!*" as the breath went out of her.

But she twisted quickly on the bed to face the danger.

There was no danger. There was merely a door—the door from stateroom to passageway—closing quickly.

Pam blinked and started to get up, and looked around the room and continued to look around it.

She saw what she had not seen before—that one of the drawers of the dressing table was partly open; that the door of one of the wardrobes stood open, too, and that clothing had been pushed on hangers to either end. Her white dinner dress—her *white* one—was lying on the floor. It would be the white one, and Pam went to pick it up.

Pam had the dress on its hanger, was herself half in the wardrobe and shielded partly by the open door,

when she heard the sound of the catch being released
on the door from passageway into stateroom.

He was coming back!

Pam looked for a weapon. She stooped and grabbed
an evening slipper—a slipper with a high, leáther heel.
It would be better than nothing, Pam thought, and
stood ready, shielding herself behind the wardrobe
door, holding the shoe as a weapon.

Surprise, Pam thought—that's my only chance. The
man's strong—he's proved that. He—

He came through the door into the stateroom. Pam,
holding the slipper high, had leaped before she
looked—had leaped and could not stop herself.

Jerry threw up a quick hand, caught the slipper
before it caught his head. With the other arm he caught
the quick, naked body of his wife.

"You," Jerry said, "are certainly impetuous today." He kicked the stateroom door closed behind
him. "But," Jerry said, "why the shoe?"

The Norths' stateroom had been searched. So had
the adjacent stateroom of the Weigands. The search
apparently had, in both cases, been quick, as if some
object of considerable size had been sought—some
object which could not be concealed under, for example, a stack of Jerry's handkerchiefs. But in both
rooms lingerie had been tumbled; in both shirts had
been turned over and, in the case of Bill Weigand's,
the laundry cardboard had been removed from all but
one.

The searcher had gone first through the Weigands'
room, Bill thought. There there had been no interruption; there drawers had been opened and closed again,

although there had been no real effort to hide the fact—except from a first casual glance—that a search had been made. Pam had, evidently, interrupted the search of her room. Trapped, the intruder had been forced to drop what he was doing and take refuge. The action was one of a badly rattled man; that it had worked to his advantage was, from his point of view, merely preposterously good luck.

The hands had been a man's hands, with a man's strength behind them. Of that, Pam North was certain. Beyond that, she could not really go.

"They looked enormous," she told Bill. "Great, hideous, groping things. But of course I was—I was rather surprised. Here I am all—all ready for a bath and and—*this* comes out of the dark. But actually, I suppose, they were just ordinary hands."

She could not really describe them further. If there had been a ring on one of the hands, or on both—if there had been a wrist watch on one or an identification bracelet on the other—well, such things would be helpful to know about. But Pam did not know.

"He turned me around," Pam said. "He—it felt as if he threw me. Of course, all he did was push." She paused. "Why only that?" she asked. "When he slugged the poor baby?"

"Chivalry," Dorian suggested. "He could see you—weren't a man."

"He certainly could," Pam said, and felt that it would be an appropriate moment to blush prettily. She waited momentarily and did not feel a proper blush. I don't blush as well as I used to, Pam thought, and sighed momentarily over lessened innocence. "He was after the things," she said then, more practically.

There could be no doubt he was after the "things,"

which was to say the effects of the late J. Orville Marsh. It had been somewhat naïve of him to think that they would have been left lying in either stateroom. They were in the purser's safe. It could only be assumed that, among the "things," there was at least one important enough to make worth while the taking of any chance, however remote.

"He took long ones," Jerry said.

Bill said, "Right," to that, and then added that the chances were not quite so long as superficially appeared. With a ship to roam, with sun to sit in, few people spend much time in staterooms, which are for the changing of clothes, the sleeping away of nights.

"Also," Bill said, "he'd probably seen us all out and around—you swimming, Pam; Jerry walking the deck; Dorian sketching on the sun deck."

"And you?" Dorian said.

"Talking to people," Bill said. "The surgeon's pretty sure young Pinkham's begun to come around—the kid's begun to babble a bit. The stewardess who found Marsh didn't see anybody behaving strangely in passageways. There's no name on the passenger list which means anything in particular to me—except Barron's. Riggs and Adjutant Jones bear Folsom out about the sword. Nobody heard the gun case being opened after midnight, although it's under—or approximately under—the windows of several staterooms. In other words—"

He was interrupted. The public-address system soothingly requested "the following to communicate with the purser—Captain and Mrs. William Weigand, Mr. and Mrs. Aaron Furstenberg; Mr. Jules Barron, Mr. Hammond Jones; Mr. J. R. Folsom." The public-address system thanked the ship as a whole and clicked.

"Cocktails with the captain," Bill said. He looked at Pam. "All he has room for at one time," Bill said.

"Humh," Pam said. "And after all the trouble I've gone to. Getting half killed. To say nothing of the risk to—"

"My head," Jerry finished for her, somewhat hurriedly.

6

The radiogram from Sergeant Stein, who had made considerable progress under circumstances which were adverse, confirmed, amplified and in some instances supplied new information. The value of the new information—and for that matter of the confirmations, the amplifications—was uncertain. Presumably, Bill Weigand thought, reading Stein's message, time would tell. Not that it always did.

Mr. and Mrs. Carl Buckley, the young couple at the captain's table—why at the captain's table? Memo to enquire—were from Emporia, Kansas. They had spent Thursday night at the Hotel Statler in New York. In Emporia, Mr. Buckley, and his father, operated The New York Haberdashery. Probably, this would eventually be filed under "Useless Information." A good many things were.

Mrs. Macklin—Mrs. Olivia Macklin—lived in New York at a residential hotel, but had lived there only for a little over two weeks. She had registered as from St. Petersburg, Florida. She had, when engaging her room—not one of the more expensive, but by most standards expensive enough—indicated her intention of staying through the winter. But on the previous Wednesday, she had reported a change in plans, and had checked out Friday morning—at 10:17—in time to go aboard the *Carib Queen*. Her daughter had not stayed with her at the hotel. The hotel had no knowledge whatever of a Miss Hilda Macklin.

Mr. and Mrs. Aaron Furstenberg occupied a large apartment in a large building on Central Park West. He had retired as a designer of jewelry three years ago; as a designer he had for many years been associated with a Fifth Avenue firm. For some years thereafter he had had his own shop on an upper floor of a building in East Fifty-seventh Street. "Very high class," Stein reported. The Furstenbergs were childless. He was around seventy; she a few years younger. They traveled a good deal.

The message added, in regard to Jules Barron, some amplification of Stein's telephoned report. Barron was a ballroom dancer, by no means a famous one. He had had no recent engagements. He was frequently seen elegantly—or at least smoothly—escorting women who tended to be older, and certainly richer, than he. The suspicion that he had other activities had been aroused only on the one occasion, and nothing had come of that. He was believed to have been born Finnegan, in Hoboken, although he was Latin in appearance. He had at one time been an instructor in one of a chain of dancing schools.

J. R. Folsom, elected Captain of the Ancient and Respectable Riflemen—an organization centering in Worcester, Massachusetts, and precisely what Folsom had said it was—was treasurer of the Worcester Paper Box Company, which had been founded by his father—R. J. Folsom. He was, as far as a quick check—and one made at night, and early Sunday morning—revealed, esteemed in the community. He was a director of the Community Chest. He was a member of the Clover Club, which was in Worcester.

Walter D. Riggs, insurance and real estate, and Hammond Jones (Buicks) also were members of the Clover Club. They were esteemed in the community. Mr. Jones had been vice-president of the Chamber of Commerce. Mr. Riggs was prominent in Rotary. They, like Folsom, were married, lived in substantial houses, and had begotten children.

And as to Marsh—

Marsh came last. There was quite a good deal of information about J. Orville Marsh, some of it merely confirming what, about Marsh, Bill Weigand already knew. Marsh was duly licensed; he had always kept his nose clean. For years he had done no divorce work. He had several times co-operated with the police, once when he had not needed to. He had never, before, got in the way—which is all that a police department can expect from a licensed private detective. There was no indication that he was in the jewelry recovery racket; he had not, of course, ever been concerned in a murder case. And, whatever he had said, he was not retired.

This had taken a little finding out. He had a small office in a good office building, with only his name on the door. There were several filing cases in it, all locked. Through the contents of the cases, two men were going slowly, carefully. They had so far found nothing to alter the official view of Marsh's activities, or nothing which seemed immediately pertinent to Marsh's death. (But what was pertinent and what was not could only be guessed at. From his distance, from the stateroom on the *Carib Queen* where Bill waited for Dorian to finish dressing, Bill could not even guess.)

Marsh's secretary, and his only employee, lived in Brooklyn. She was thin and gray and fifty-five, and had been Marsh's secretary for twenty years. Told Marsh was dead, her eyes had gone blank, as if she had been struck. But she had steadied herself quickly. She had then been precise and careful—so precise, so careful, that much patience was required of Stein, who had done this one himself, and Detective O'Grady, working with him. Bill Weigand could read this between the lines. She had been insistent on the confidential aspect of Marsh's trade; on her obligation to preserve that confidence. So, it was by no means certain that she had told them all she knew, or all that might prove pertinent.

Stein had radioed at considerable length concerning Marsh's secretary, who was named, rather unexpectedly, Miss Perky. It had been, Bill gathered, some years since the name had been descriptive, if it once had been. It was evident that Miss Perky had interested Stein. He would see her again. Meanwhile—it could be assumed that Marsh was not retired.

One current case, Miss Perky admitted to, although Stein thought she had told as little as she could manage. Marsh had been, when he went aboard the *Carib Queen*—"but that was merely a vacation"—engaged in a search for a Mrs. Winifred Ferris. Mrs. Ferris was—even this came grudgingly—"middle aged." Pressed to be more specific, Miss Perky had failed to be. She had never met the woman. How could she have met her, since she was missing? She had never seen a photograph of Mrs. Ferris. That sort of thing was not her job. Who had retained Marsh to search for her?

She had considered that, sitting in her small, plainly neat, apartment in the Bay Ridge section of Brooklyn. She had, finally, decided that that fact was not, in itself, confidential. She had said she "understood" Mrs. Ferris's children had engaged Mr. Marsh. She did not, she said, know the names of the children. She did not, she said, know where the children lived. Stein had pointed out, with increasing firmness, that her responsibility now—whatever it had been in the past—was to co-operate with the police.

She had insisted she did not know—that there had been no correspondence relative to Mrs. Ferris, that Mr. Marsh kept confidential matters confidential, even from her. But she would, finally, say this much:

On the previous Wednesday, Marsh had made a trip to Boston. She had got his parlor car reservation. She had gathered that it was in regard to the Ferris matter, since Marsh had said it was business, and since—she thought, could not be sure—the Ferris matter was the only one in which he had been, currently, engaged. Leaving the office to catch a midday train to Boston on Wednesday, Marsh had told her that she would not, probably, see him again until he returned from the cruise. He had, she thought, planned to catch the midnight train from Boston Thursday night, pick up what he wanted from his hotel, and go, then, to the ship.

She had debated with herself again, and had finally decided that it was not confidential that Mr. Marsh had made up his mind to go on the cruise only the previous Tuesday. Telephoning to make a reservation at so late a date, she had at first been told that it would be impossible. But later the travel agency had called back to say that, if Mr. Marsh would take a double state-room—at one and a half times the two in a room rate—he could be accommodated. He had agreed to that, Stein thought rather to Miss Perky's surprise.

Stein had found five subscribers named Ferris in the Worcester telephone book. They were being checked out to discover whether any had a mother missing.

The secretary of the Clover Club had reported, resignedly, that half the members indecipherably signed their names. Show him the signature, and he would identify it. Bill Weigand sighed. He looked out the porthole, with some resentment, at the shining blue water which so implacably separated him from things that needed doing. The Clover Club had some two hundred members. One of the things which might turn out to need doing was to enquire of each whether he had employed one J. Orville Marsh, private detective. And the members might reasonably feel it was nobody's business but their own.

Dorian reported herself ready for cocktails with the captain. She looked it, in a white piqué dress, fitting closely down to the waist, flaring below it, with high-heeled blue linen slippers on slender feet. They went by the purser's bureau on their way to the captain's quarters, although the bureau was not on the way. They were the first in Captain Cunningham's office-sitting room, which was according to plan. Bill Weigand had time for a brief conference with the captain, which was also as planned. Another steward, older than Cholly, supplied cocktails, poured Captain Cunningham a glass of sherry.

Folsom and Hammond Jones came. Folsom was not in uniform—he wore a dark, double-breasted business suit, and his plump, ruddy face was set in a serious pattern—gave the effect of being double-breasted, too. Mr. Jones was sparer, and in uniform—and still, indefinably, like Folsom. Captain Cunningham told them both it was good of them to come and when Folsom waited, as if for more, merely smiled pleasantly and asked what they would have to drink. Folsom had bourbon on the rocks; Jones, scotch and ginger ale. It was, Bill thought, a credit to British composure that Captain Cunningham did not wince at that, and that the steward said, merely, "Thank you, sir."

The Furstenbergs came next, and met the others with dignity, as if, in their lengthening lives, they had met people of many kinds, and met all with tolerance. Furstenberg's rather heavy face was moderated by a courteous half smile. He wore a dark suit of Italian silk, beautifully cut. He wore rimless glasses, to which a black ribbon was looped. His wife was, within the restraints of dignity, cheerful, in face and in manner. Bill made mental comparisons, and found it extremely unlikely that she could be the original of the photograph Marsh had carried. The lines of her face were upward lines; those in the photograph drooped sadly. The Furstenbergs asked for sherry.

Jules Barron was the last to come. He wore slacks of a yellowish hue, and sandals; he wore a jacket of soft brick red, slightly broad of shoulder, and a scarf, in lieu of necktie, to match the jacket. He was a handsome youngish man, black haired and—dashing. The word, with all its implications, came trotting to the mind.

But for all this, Jules Barron somewhat lacked assurance—seemed a little surprised to find himself there. That Folsom should show himself wary—should look from time to time at Bill Weigand, and away again quickly; at Captain Cunningham and as quickly away again—was to be expected. Captain Folsom suspected something was up, and had reason to. Folsom, understandably, might fear that he was about to be sneaked up on. But Mr. Barron had no obvious reason to feel uneasy.

It was possible, Bill thought, smiling rejection of another cocktail, that Barron merely did not see quite where he fitted in. Folsom and Jones were mature businessmen; the Furstenbergs even more mature and of a world which Jules Barron probably did not frequent. (It was difficult to imagine the Furstenbergs at a night club—as difficult as it was easy to imagine them at Carnegie Hall.) It was, faintly, difficult to imagine Barron out of a night club.

And it was likely also, Bill thought—while agreeing with Hammond Jones that great strides were being made by the automobile industry, and in particular by General Motors—that Barron missed suitable women. Admittedly, the small pre-luncheon cocktail party in the master's quarters of the *Carib Queen* was not too well assorted. The expression of Jules Barron brightened as he looked on Dorian Weigand, as did the expressions of most men, but there was, clearly, only one of her, and that one, as evidently, attached. Mrs. Furstenberg brought out a good deal of charm in Jules Barron, but that, Bill assumed, was reflexive. Mr. Barron might, in short, reasonably wonder why he was there at all.

And the others, also, might feel that Captain Cunningham gave somewhat odd parties—that he was either an inexperienced or a careless host. But that was a chance that had had to be taken, if anything was to come of the party. It was probable that nothing was.

"As to this talk about too much horsepower," Jones said, "that's a lot of malarkey. Get in a jam on the road, and if you don't have it, where are you? I'd like to have them answer that."

Bill Weigand agreed he had a point. He continued to listen, to nod encouragement, as Mr. Jones progressed. He learned, not to his surprise, that the manufacturers put a lot of pressure on dealers and what part of the anatomy that sometimes gave a pain in. He listened, also, to the others—to the captain telling Mrs. Furstenberg that he was sure she would enjoy Havana; to Dorian's few words as she listened, with an attention which only a husband could doubt, to Folsom's description of his son's wedding. Folsom showed pictures of it, now. And Folsom's uneasiness had, apparently, diminished. Mrs. Furstenberg was being charmed by Mr. Barron, and taking it well.

Captain Cunningham gave his attention to Aaron Furstenberg. There was another round of drinks—now it was only a pleasant small party; a service of the *Carib Queen* for those to be especially honored, for those on the captain's little list. Still listening to Hammond Jones—who was now evaluating other automatic transmission as against Dynaflow—Bill Weigand nevertheless caught Captain Cunningham's eye. Almost imperceptibly, Bill nodded.

"Speaking of jewels," Captain Cunningham said, and just as imperceptibly raised his voice. "Got something here I'd like to show you. Pick your brains, what?" Furstenberg sat near him, but the captain's voice was still raised a little. "Got them here somewhere," Cunningham said, and reached out to a drawer of his desk, and looked into it, and shook his head and tried another. "Here we are," he said. "What do you think of these, Mr. Furstenberg?"

He held four photographs out to Aaron Furstenberg—four glossy photographs of bracelet, necklaces, ring set with a single large stone.

"Wife's great-aunt," Cunningham said. "Left her these. Tell us they're valuable. Only, I'm not sure I trust this solicitor chap. Know what I mean?"

Bill Weigand did not think anyone was likely to know what Captain Cunningham meant. That was all right, too.

"What I mean is," Cunningham said. "Sell them there, through this solicitor chap? Or have them shipped to the States, sell them there? Not the sort of thing my old girl would think suitable to wear around, y'know." He paused. "Harumph," he said.

The captain, Bill decided, was being carried away by his role. Apparently the British, too, read Wodehouse. Bill shook his head slightly, thinking Cunningham might be on the verge of a second "Harumph."

"Appreciate your advice," Captain Cunningham said to Aaron Furstenberg, and permitted himself a small sip from his glass of sherry. He nodded, just perceptibly, assurance toward Bill Weigand.

If Furstenberg was surprised at this intrusion of business on a social gathering, he was too courteous to show surprise. He did not, in fact, show anything. He took the photographs and looked at them with care, holding them so that the light fell first from one direction, and then another. Bill watched him; he managed also to watch the others.

Folsom, in midstream, ended his flow of family reminiscence. He watched Furstenberg turn the photographs in manicured fingers.

The captain's slightly raised voice had done it. Other conversation stopped; Aaron Furstenberg's study of the photographs became the center of attention. Bill leaned back in his chair, looking at the others—looking at Folsom, at Hammond Jones. He looked, also and quickly, at Jules Barron. The handsome young man, so Latin for a man born Finnegan, was leaning forward in his chair, his attitude one of interested attention. Folsom's face and attitude were more revealing, which was understandable. Whatever he knew—and he might know nothing beyond the fact that J. Orville Marsh was dead with a sword wound in his chest—J. R. Folsom did not believe in Cunningham's wife's great-aunt. It was Folsom's understandable belief that something was up. Jones, so far as Bill could determine, showed merely the polite interest due a host's concerns.

"They appear," Furstenberg said, in a soft voice, a voice carefully modulated, "to be very nice pieces. Probably of considerable value. Of course, from photographs—" He did not bother to say the obvious. He did not seem surprised that Captain Cunningham had not seen the obvious.

"Oh," Cunningham said, "imagine they're real enough. Old girl wasn't the type to wear paste. Have to give her that."

They gave her that, sight unseen.

"Quite," Furstenberg said. "I hadn't meant precisely that, captain. But the value of gems varies a great deal with their character. Entirely aside from their size. No one could appraise from photographs."

"Oh," Cunningham said. "I realize that, of course. Hadn't expected an appraisal. But—probably worth quite a bit, aren't they?"

"I should," Furstenberg said, "imagine they would be worth a good many thousands, captain. In dollars— or in pounds. But—they'll be officially appraised, of course. By your tax people." He looked at the photographs again, politely. "I shouldn't imagine it will make much difference whether they are sold in London or New York," he said, and held the photographs out.

And as he did so, Jules Barron leaned still more forward in his chair.

"Mind if I have a look, captain?" Bill said, and reached out for the photographs, and was told that, certainly, the captain did not mind. Bill took the familiar photographs and studied them. He produced a low whistle of admiration.

"They look," Bill said, "like a lot of money. Wouldn't you say so, Mr. Barron?"

And he held the photographs out to Barron, whose hands seemed eager for them. Barron looked quickly. He did not look long at any of the pictured pretty things, and there was no change in the expression on his face—there was, indeed, no expression readable on his face. He handed the pictures back.

"Do to me," he said, and then drew his lips into a smile. "Not that I know much about things like that."

"Oh," Bill Weigand said, "nor I. You interested in jewelry, Mr. Folsom? Mr. Jones?"

Folsom took the photographs—he took them a little as if he expected they might be hot. He looked at them and said that to him, too, they looked like money. He looked up at Bill Weigand and his eyes seemed slightly puzzled. He looked again at the pictured bracelet, and handed the photographs to Hammond Jones, who looked longer and said he wished his wife had that kind of a great-aunt and handed the pictures on. Mrs. Furstenberg looked at them, and said that they were beautiful, and Dorian looked at them and said they certainly were and handed them back to Captain Cunningham. And then the public-address system, with chimes, announced the second sitting.

Jules Barron was first on his feet—he was on them almost too quickly for a suave young man who, it could be presumed, lived by charm. He seemed to realize this, belatedly, and then smiled very charmingly around, and said, "The sea air, sir," to Captain Cunningham. Then he thanked the captain, and smiled at all, and went.

"Well?" Captain Cunningham said to Bill, who with Dorian had lingered after the others.

"Mr. Folsom," Bill said, "has an uneasy mind. Which may be merely because he knows more than the others. Barron was interested in the pictures, I thought. And in rather a hurry to get away."

"Quite," Captain Cunningham said. "I thought that. Except—"

"Right," Bill said, "except that he satisfied his interest with a couple of glances."

"Which means?"

"I haven't any real idea," Bill said. "But his interest was—interesting."

"We don't," Captain Cunningham said, "seem to make any very great progress."

"Early days," Bill said. "By the way, captain—did your wife have a great-aunt?"

"Had," Cunningham said. "And, has. Sprightly old girl. Poor as a church mouse, unfortunately. You'll want these back?"

Bill took the photographs, in an envelope. He took them back to the purser's safe.

Left out of things, and with Pam feeling it—after all, who had taken the greater risks?—the Norths had gone to the smoke room for a pre-luncheon drink. Pam wore a sleeveless yellow dress of linen. "Look," she said, and held her arms out in front of her, over the table. "Bruises. Where he grabbed me."

Jerry looked. He looked very carefully. It was possible that Pam's upper arms were reddened somewhat where the hands had held, and pushed. It was only possible. Jerry told Pam that, in all probability, she would live. The steward came, and he ordered martinis, "Very dry with a twist of lemon peel," the steward said, unprompted. "And he's not to drop the peel in." The steward looked pleased with himself. His was *Carib Queen* service.

"Quite," Jerry said.

"It was funny about Mrs. Macklin," Pam said. "Why me?"

"I'm afraid," Jerry said, "you've dropped a stitch. What was funny about Mrs. Macklin? And you?"

She thought she had told him. She did now. Told, Jerry could not explain why Mrs. Macklin, in her search for Detective Marsh, had come to Pam. He agreed with Pam's suggestion that it would have been more reasonable to go to someone in authority— perhaps the purser. Presumably, pursers were around to keep track of passengers. But it was, from what they had seen of her, too much to expect that Mrs. Macklin would be reasonable. It was even quite possible that Mrs. Macklin had been a little drunk.

"She had a pink scarf with that hair of hers," Pam admitted. "Still—at first I did think she probably was, but then that she wasn't. Merely peculiar. She must be, to pick that color."

"Pink?" Jerry said.

Pink too, Pam agreed. Although she had been thinking primarily of the red. It was not an especially good red—particularly for hair.

The drinks came. They were dry and cold, but the lemon peel had been dropped in. The point is one about which bartenders are adamant.

"One thing," Pam said, after her first sip, "it eliminates Mrs. Macklin. She wouldn't be looking for him if she'd killed him. At least, not on deck."

"You'd had an eye on her?" Jerry asked.

"On everybody," Pam said. "Haven't you? Although a sword's too long for a woman. How long is a sword, by the way?"

They varied, Jerry thought, out of a considerable ignorance of swords. This ône looked to be about thirty inches—in a straight line which, actually, it did not follow. He thought that, more than the length, the physical strength needed to push it into a man argued against a woman.

"Unless the ship helped," Pam said, and Jerry looked at her blankly. "By rolling," Pam said. "Or pitching, I suppose. With that, anybody could merely—well, lurch a sword into somebody. The way it was when we were dancing."

Jerry saw, then. He said he saw. The *Carib Queen* now seemed almost without movement, and yet liquid moved in their glasses; just perceptibly, the wall they faced across the room seemed to rise, then slowly to decline. There had been rather more movement the previous night.

But the point was academic, Pam said, at least insofar as it concerned Mrs. Macklin. Because it was obvious that— She stopped, because Jerry was shaking his head slowly. "Oh," Pam North said, "I didn't think of that. Of course. I'd be supposed to pass it on."

If they wanted to make Mrs. Macklin, against all evidence, into a reasonable person they would, Jerry agreed, have to consider the possibility—the obvious possibility that by asking about Marsh, Mrs. Macklin would supply prima-facie evidence that she had not done away with him. Since, as Pam said, if you have run a sword through a man, you do not look around a ship for him.

And also, Mrs. Macklin might well be fishing—trying to find out what was going on or, rather, why nothing did seem to be going on.

"You'd feel let down," Pam said, "if you killed a man and nobody noticed it."

Jerry agreed that one might well. The anti-climax would be— He stopped, since he was no longer being listened to. Pam was looking up the room, toward the doors which led into it from the Grand Entrance forward. Miss Hilda Macklin was coming into the smoke room. She came with a kind of uncertainty, as if doubtful of her welcome. She wore the gray linen suit which did so little for her, who had, hidden under it, so much to be done for. She was alone, and it was apparent that she was looking for someone.

"Mother, dear mother, come home with me now," Jerry said, under his breath, and Pam nodded that she was afraid so. But Hilda saw the Norths and, if there was nothing in her face to show that her confidence was restored, her pace was quickened. She came to their table, and Jerry stood up. And Hilda said, in a small, uncertain voice, "I hate to bother you. But I'm—I'm worried."

They looked at her, and looked blanky. And, blankly, Jerry said, "Won't you sit down?"

She did, irresolutely. She said she was Hilda Macklin. Pam said, with what reassurance she could put into so simple a statement, that they were the Norths.

"I know," Hilda Macklin said. "I—I asked someone. I've been trying to get up courage." She stopped with that, apparently having failed in her attempt. Jerry asked her if she would have a drink and she said, "No," and then, almost at once, "Could I have a sherry?" She could; with the aid of the steward she did. She said, too anxiously, "Oh. Thank you" and sipped from the glass. They waited.

"Mother was talking to you this morning," Hilda said, finally, and the words came in a rush. "She—she seemed so excited. I—I was afraid she was bothering you, Mrs. North. And that you wouldn't understand. Did she—bother you?"

"No," Pam said. "I don't know quite what you mean, Miss Macklin. She didn't bother me at all. She just—just wanted to know whether I'd seen Mr. Marsh."

"Mr. Marsh?" Hilda repeated. "He's—oh, I remember. I heard something about him. He's a detective, isn't he? And—why did she ask you that? Did she say?"

"Something about hiring him," Pam said. "To find out who had searched her stateroom. Yours too, I suppose it is."

"Oh dear," Hilda said. "Oh *dear*. I was afraid it was that." She put the palms of her hands against her forehead, as if to hide behind them. She took them down again.

She took a sip from her glass, as if, again, she sought courage.

"I may as well tell you," she said, and spoke quickly, as if she snatched at courage. "There wasn't anybody. Nobody searched our room. She just—she makes things up. When she's been—" She paused. "She's dear and sweet other times." She paused again. She looked at Pam intently, then at Jerry. "I hate to have to tell people," she said. "But—she's not responsible, sometimes. Not really. I hoped—I hoped getting her away would help. Where everything was peaceful. That she'd relax and—" She spread her hands hopelessly. She had slender hands with pointed fingers, the nails short and unrouged.

There did not seem to be anything to say. But it did not appear that Hilda Macklin expected anything to be said.

"I—I hate to have to talk like this," Hilda said. "To go around—well, it really comes to going around warning people. Not to take mother too seriously. Now—this Mr. Marsh. I'll have to find him and—" She did not finish. Instead, she stood up.

"I'm terribly sorry," she said. "Terribly sorry about everything. Bothering you this way—and her bothering you and—and everything. You've—"

Again she left it unfinished. She merely shook her head, and walked away from the table, straight—straight as a broomstick, one would have thought—under the shapeless suit. The Norths watched her; looked at each other.

"The poor thing," Pam said. "The poor, poor thing."

Jerry North raised his eyebrows.

"I suppose so," he said. "But—why? Why make so much of it? So—"

"You don't know anything," Pam said. "Not anything at all. About women."

"Probably not," Jerry said, and raised his eyebrows again, but this time at the steward, who hovered near. The steward went briskly off.

"How dreadful it is for a girl like that," Pam said. "To have a mother like that. And those clothes. I—I could cry."

But she did not, and when the steward returned she only momentarily looked with doubt at the glass which held a second martini.

"After all," Pam said, "we're on vacation. And that poor girl. And you are a man, of course."

"Only," Jerry said, providing the missing word.

7

The Norths had almost empty glasses when Bill and Dorian joined them. Bill told them of the cocktail party in the captain's quarters; of the display of pictures and the reactions to them. He was told, by Norths working in relays, of Hilda Macklin's apology for, explanation of, her mother. Pam added a few comments on the misbehavior of parents who batten on their young.

"Obviously," Pam said, "the poor thing hasn't any life to call her own. And her mother picks her clothes just to be—mean." Pam paused. "And," she said, "she's what people call a 'bad' drinker. I never saw worse."

Nobody argued against that.

The Norths finished their last sips. The four went aft, in the sunshine of the boat deck, and down to the dining saloon. The plaice was very naice. Jules Barron, although he had been first to leave the captain's quarters, and then had implied hunger, was late in reaching his table. The four at the table so conveniently—as it had turned out—near by were well into vichyssoise, preliminary to plaice. ("The motto of our

111

steward," Pam North said, "is 'Let 'em heat fish.' ")
Folsom had been in his chair when the Norths and
Weigands arrived, and had looked lonely at the big
table, separated from the first officer, its only other
occupant, by the empty chair of J. Orville Marsh. Mrs.
Macklin—who unexpectedly wore a tweed suit—and
Hilda, who wore a limp dress of no particular color,
were later than Barron, and Captain Cunningham did
not appear at all. It was probably, Pam thought, that
he had had enough of everybody. Unless, of course, it
was his turn to steer the ship. . . .

It was very warm, very bright, on the promenade
deck, aft, and for half an hour they reclined, torpid, and
digested plaice. Jerry said, sleepily, that he ought to
walk, and did not. Dorian said that, if it came to
activity, she had a sketch half finished, and did nothing
about it. Pam said it tired her merely to listen to them
and Bill Weigand said nothing whatever, and appeared
to be asleep.

But he did not sleep long. A steward came to him,
bent politely and spoke into his ear. Bill said, "Right,"
and, to the others, "Stein's calling," and went. Afterward, Dorian stretched, suavely as a cat, or almost,
and went for sketch pad. "I really ought to get some
exercise," Jerry told himself, and Pam, and shifted his
position slightly in a deck chair. And one man said to
another, behind the Norths, "What I hear is, somebody fell overboard."

"The way I hear it," the other man said, "some
woman shot herself."

It had started; here was evidence that it had started.
It had been, for all the discretion enjoined on Captain
Cunningham—practiced insofar as was possible—in-
evitable that it would start. And now it eddied through

the ship—moved softly, changing as it moved, from deck chair to deck chair. At the bar it passed, in multiple forms, from Respectable Rifleman to Respectable Rifleman, as they stood shoulder to shoulder. It swirled softly among the tables in the smoke room, and among those—generally older, and more sedate—who frequented the Grand Lounge, from which windows, high above the ship's hull, opened to the sea. It swirled more rapidly in the small cocktail lounge off the dining saloon. In the motion picture theater which opened off A Deck, it was more exciting than the movie. It took new forms in the crew's quarters, and the kitchen was full of it.

The ship, steaming prettily into ever warmer waters, suffused with rumor. This was rather pleasant than otherwise for the hundred and forty-odd passengers. It is not always that, to the *divertissements* offered on a pleasure cruise, the spice of mysterious violence is thus generously added. The managing director of the line had been wrong. Everybody enjoyed it very much, although nobody knew quite what "it" was.

Where it had begun, nobody knew that afternoon, or could find out later. Nobody made great effort; once rumor began, its point of origin became of little importance. Perhaps Stewardess Felicia Brown, although she had been warned, could not restrain dark hints to Mrs. Palsey and Mrs. Fish and young Miss Pratt, the flibbertigibbet, when they met in their crowded cabin below decks. Perhaps an assistant purser, overwhelmed with knowledge so dramatic, had let some of it trickle to his friends. Perhaps, while he could still talk—he could not, yet, talk again—young Cholly had talked too much.

By the time strangers were telling strangers, and so

engendering that relaxed good fellowship so to be prized on holiday, the rumor would not have been recognized by its maker. That somebody had fallen overboard was, inevitably, the simplest version, and the one most often repeated. It became known for a fact, by those who did not have other and more factual facts, that the ship had, during the night, in darkness, turned back on its course in search of a—it was to be hoped—floating passenger. The floater, but by now sinker (since the fact was that the search had been hopeless from the start), was that blond girl who is always in the swimming pool, the poor man with a mourning band around his arm (in his case it had been suicide) and that little boy of seven who was always running into people. (A small, but darkly determined, group stuck to this theory to the end, and told friends afterward in New York that it had happened and was, if anything, too good for him.)

But it was also a fact that the dark man in B 29 had killed the woman he was traveling with, and it was all very well to say she had been his wife, but if you really wanted to know the truth— And the chief bar steward had hanged himself. That was why nobody had seen him for hours. And the staff captain had throttled Miss Springer, the social hostess. But it was really one of the girls in the group of entertainers—the one who tried to sing like Dinah Shore, and so noticeably failed—who had been throttled. By the man who played the piano. On the other hand, it wasn't violent death at all. People would believe *anything*. For those who really wanted to know it was—whisper, whisper. And, whisper, whisper. "But how *dreadful*," they said in the Grand Lounge, over teacups. "Sort of thing that happens all the time," they told one another, man to man, in the smoke room.

Now and then they came closer. It was that New York policeman with the pretty wife—the one who pretended he was merely on vacation. Actually he was after a gangster, who was on the ship in disguise, and he had been killed by the gangster—a big gambling man from Chicago. No, *he* had killed the *gangster*. It was being hushed up. The body—whose ever body it was—was in the meat refrigerator. No, it was in one of the freezers. No—all it really came to was: there had been an outbreak of typhus—no, beriberi—in the crew. The captain's steward, the one who waited on the captain's table, had died of it. That's why you didn't see *him* any more.

Rumor was a haze in the *Carib Queen*—a haze in public rooms and passageways and in staterooms. Warm breezes across boat deck and sun deck did not blow the haze away. Respected Captain J. R. Folsom, about three o'clock, groped his way through it to stand, as if by accident, near the Norths, who still reclined. Jerry, all thought of exercise abandoned, did not even twitch. It was with some difficulty that he opened his eyes when the respected captain, somewhat morosely, said, "Good afternoon."

"Huh?" Jerry said, as Pam, who had been oiling said, "Isn't it a pretty one?"

"Oh," Jerry said. "Afternoon, captain." He moved his feet, invitingly. Folsom sat down on the end of the deck chair. He wore a bright sports shirt, and slacks of green. His face was red, from nature and from sun. But the gaiety of color did not, it seemed, reach his eyes, which were coldly gray—if a little bloodshot. Jerry's deck chair gave somewhat under Folsom's stocky weight.

"Hear something's happened," Folsom said. "You hear what it was?"

They had heard several of the versions. Jerry hesitated.

"Yes," Pam said. "We know what it was, Mr. Folsom."

Folsom said, "Oh." Then he said, "Supposed you did. Being with this policeman and everything. Although they told *me* to keep it under my hat."

He continued to look at them, still with vestiges of doubt.

"Mr. Marsh," Pam said. "He was killed with your sword."

"Wait a minute," Folsom said. "What do you mean 'my sword'?"

"Used to cut your son's wedding cake," Pam said. "Wasn't it yours?"

"The company's," Folsom said. He looked sad. "Don't know that it matters much," he said. "Just keeping the record straight, like they say." He paused. "Since you know," he said, "I suppose you know about me? That I went along to find him and blundered into things? When he didn't show up for a drink?"

"Yes," Jerry said.

"Been trying to remember," Folsom said. "Weren't you in the bar last night? Before the dining room opened?" He snapped his fingers. "Bought you a drink," he said, with triumph. "Standing there with the poor guy and said to myself, 'There's a nice couple. Buy them a drink.'" He shook his head. "Couple of hours later," he said, "he was dead, the poor guy. Makes you think."

They agreed it made them think. Folsom mopped his forehead with a handkerchief.

"What gets you," Folsom said, "I figured him for a hundred per cent. Never happened to run into a man in his line of work. Know the police commissioner at home, of course. Shows up at Rotary, like everybody else. But what they call a private eye."

He looked at them, and again he shook his head, as if all of it—the fact that a man may be dead only hours after one talks to him; that people may not fit into the patterns one cuts for them—bewildered him entirely.

Only—Pam North thought. Only—his eyes really aren't like that at all. Not when he forgets to be one hundred per cent Rotarian. But she stopped herself, thinking that now she was doing it. She was trying to push people into patterns she had shaped for them. What do I know about Rotarians? Pam asked herself, and was answered by dead silence. Perhaps all of them have shrewd gray eyes.

"Read about them in books," Folsom said. "You know, Marsh didn't even carry a gun. Told me that. Know how sometimes you meet a guy and get to talking? Say more, maybe, than you would to some guy you'd known all your life? Learn a lot that way. Bet he knows—" He stopped. "Bet he heard more, anyway, about paper boxes than he'd ever heard."

They both nodded their heads, it not being apparent that they were expected to speak.

"One thing he told me," Folsom said. "He'd been letting on he was retired. Well, he wasn't. He was here—right here on this boat—to try to find somebody. A woman, I gathered. This Captain Weigand of yours know about that?"

Now his gray eyes were suddenly very sharp and shrewd indeed.

"Because I was thinking," Folsom said, without waiting for an answer. "Suppose a man in his business finds somebody who doesn't want to be found?"

He looked at them expectantly—as, Pam thought, one might who had planted a seed and was waiting for it to come up.

"The point would be," Pam North said, "had he? Did he say he had?"

"He didn't *say* he had," Folsom told them. "He didn't really say anything. Just—let things drop. I'll admit I had to put two and two together. But, he admitted I was right. Said he could see I was the kind of man you couldn't keep things from." He paused. "Shouldn't repeat that," he said. "I don't pretend to be any smarter than the next fellow, if you know what I mean."

"Oh," Pam said, "I do, Mr. Folsom. And you and Mr. Marsh got quite friendly?"

"Fellow was at loose ends," Folsom said. "You could see that. Wanted somebody to talk to." He nodded his head; he mopped it. "Something I will say," he did say, "I'm an easy man to talk to. Get *along* with people."

"Oh," Pam said. "I'm sure you do. I—"

She was interrupted. A rifleman, in full regalia—and looking well steamed—stood at attention in front of Folsom, white-gloved hands stiffly at the seams of trousers.

"Sir," he said. "Sergeant Montgomery reporting, sir."

"Inspect—gloves," Folsom said, standing himself. Sergeant Montgomery brought his hands forward smartly, palms up. The gloves appeared to be immaculate.

"Carry on," Folsom said, and was saluted, and returned the salute. "In a military manner," Folsom added. "And not the whole time in the bar."

"Sir," Montgomery said, and did an about-face and

went off with measured tread. Folsom looked after him. "Good man," he said. "Hundred per cent. Well—bothered you people enough."

"Not at all," Jerry said, but he stood up.

"Tell your policeman about it," Folsom said. "If you think it might mean anything."

"Oh, we will," Pam said, and Mr. Folsom said, "Well" once more, and went off, not with measured tread.

"Well," Pam said, when he had gone off far enough, "isn't he the subtle one?"

He could not, necessarily, be blamed, Jerry pointed out. Folsom had blundered into things. It was possible he was merely trying to blunder out again. The most innocent man might well. As for the woman—there was a picture of a woman.

"Which he's afraid we might miss," Pam agreed. "Oh, I don't doubt Mr. Marsh told him something. Perhaps even showed him the picture. Only—why?"

"Captain Folsom is an easy man to talk to," Jerry reminded her. "Says so himself, as he shouldn't. He starts talking to Marsh and—"

Pam shook her head. She said it hadn't sounded that way. It sounded as if Marsh had been the one who had started it, and had opened the conversation. And again—why?

"Wanted somebody to talk to," Jerry told her. "As Folsom says. As a matter of fact, Marsh talked freely enough to us."

"You pumped," Pam said. "To see if you could bring up a book. And—he didn't tell us anything about looking for a missing woman. Here, I mean."

"Folsom," Jerry said, "gets along with people. Says so himself."

"On the other hand," Pam said, "did you think that Marsh may have been pumping him?"

Jerry had not. "About paper boxes?" he asked.

He was told that it was all very well, but that there might be more than met the eye.

The Cambridge police had found the daughter and son and daughter-in-law of Mrs. Winifred Ferris—found them living in a substantial house in Cambridge, and sorry to hear about the death of J. Orville Marsh (who had seemed such a nice man, and so different from what one would have expected) and quite sure that the disappearance of their mother and mother-in-law could have had nothing to do with it. Not that they hadn't employed Mr. Marsh to find her. But—she had been found.

"Back home?" Bill Weigand asked, and Sergeant Stein, his voice crackling with static—and now and then whistling curiously—said that it hadn't come to that. She was in California, and planning to stay there, and she had written her family to say so. Stein amplified, relaying the report of the Boston police.

Mrs. Winifred Ferris—age sixty-six, height five feet six, weight one hundred and seventy, white hair—had left the Cambridge house about four months earlier. They had wakened one morning and found her gone, with a note left. She had said that she wasn't going to be a burden any longer, but that they were not to worry about her, because she was perfectly able to take care of herself.

"Money?" Bill asked, and was told by Stein that they said so; that there seemed, had seemed to the Cambridge police, to be plenty of money in the Ferris family.

The son and daughter, and daughter-in-law, had

expected her to return. They did not admit it—and the police were in no position to press enquiries—but the detectives who had talked to them thought that this was probably not Mrs. Ferris's first disappearance. But when time passed, and she did not return, they had engaged Marsh to look for her.

"Not to bring her back," Stein said. "Just so they could know where she was. That's what they say."

Marsh had—or thought he had—traced her to Arizona, but there lost the trail. He had, nevertheless, continued a search until about a week previously, when a letter had come from her in California—a very pleasant letter, the police were told, one assuring everybody that she was well, and happy, and liked the climate and had made some wonderful friends and thought California was much better for her than the Boston area.

"No doubt about the letter?" Bill asked.

"They say not. Her handwriting. Her—the way she usually wrote. Looks as if we wash it out."

"Nothing fishy about it?" Bill asked.

"I didn't see them," Stein said. "I'm just passing it along. The boys in Cambridge don't seem to have smelled fish."

"Somebody could have mailed the letter for her," Bill said. "But—" He let it hang. "Did they happen to get a picture of her? I suppose, if it looked okay, they didn't."

They had not.

"Fingerprints?" Bill asked, and for a moment static crackled back at him. Then Stein said, "You don't give up easily. No. No place to get them. The letter's gone. Her room's been redecorated. No prints on file."

"Where in California?" Bill asked then, and was told Los Angeles—merely Los Angeles.

"And that's not fishy?" Bill said.

Stein was, again, merely a relay point. He had, of course, brought it up. The Cambridge police didn't think it fishy. The Ferris family did not think it fishy. Mrs. Winifred Ferris wanted them to know she was all right; she did not want them to bother her. "A case," Stein said, "of don't call me. I'll call you. It could be, captain."

"Right," Bill said. "It could. By the way, has she any other children?"

She had not.

There was nothing new—from Marsh's files. There was nothing new from Worcester.

Stein had suggested he fly to Worcester. Higher authority—in the person of Deputy Chief Inspector Artemus O'Malley—had snorted, had enquired who was supposed to pay; had pointed out that the *Carib Queen* was of British registry, so that her crimes became British. (O'Malley actually said "English" and said it with asperity.) When he had more to go on—specifically a radioed picture of the signature— Stein would take the point up again.

"As soon as we get in," Bill promised. "I'll send the picture of the woman, too. Have Cambridge try it for size."

"You don't give up at all," Stein said. "And, suppose it is? We already know he was looking for her. Had been, anyway."

"Right," Bill said. "All the same."

Stein promised, needlessly, that they would keep at it. Bill replaced the telephone receiver and looked at it reproachfully. He went to the doctor's office, and was taken to the infirmary, where Cholly Pinkham lay in bed, conscious—and extremely embarrassed. Asked how he felt, he admitted to a headache. Asked what he could tell, he became more embarrassed than ever.

"Let you down, cap'n," he said. "The old man, too."

Because, he remembered nothing—at any rate, remembered nothing useful. He had lain down on one of the beds, in the darkness, determined to keep awake. He had waked up, an hour or so ago, where he was now. Between, there was nothing. It worried young Cholly; it frightened him a little.

"Perfectly natural," the doctor told him. "You got knocked about, son. Knocked it out of you."

"Let everybody down," Cholly said, and was disconsolate. They left him so.

"Concussion," the ship's surgeon said, needlessly, when they were outside. "Wipes things out, sometimes."

Bill knew that. Would what had been wiped out return? The physician could only shrug, only point out that time would tell.

"I'd like someone with him tonight," Bill said. "To see he isn't—bothered."

"That way, is it?" the physician said and, when Bill said it might be, said he would pass the word. "It's all a sticky business," the doctor said, and Bill agreed it was indeed, and went to look at the gun cases, inboard on the promenade deck, forward on the starboard side—just where a promenader, making a clockwise circuit, might most easily bark shins on them. The cases were chests, somewhat larger than coffins. They were both padlocked.

They stood under the windows of promenade deck staterooms. The occupants of at least three rooms could look almost directly down on them, those in another could peer out, at angles, and see the chests, if they wanted to go to the trouble. There did not seem to be any reason why they should or why Bill Weigand, having seen that there appeared to be nothing to see, should stand in front of the boxes and look down at them as, in fact, he had done before. Now he was not really seeing the chests; he was simply, not too happily, wondering where—where the hell—he went next. This uncertainty sometimes afflicts detectives, as it does others. It is, of course, nothing to reveal in the presence of possible malefactors.

Standing so bemused, looking at nothing in particular, Bill Weigand began to feel that odd, largely intangible, creeping sensation which sometimes results from being surreptitiously looked at. Bill did not immediately alter his position; he tried, more practically, to determine, without himself moving, from what direction he might, subconsciously, have noted movement. Presumably from the windows of one of the staterooms which overlooked the gun cases.

Bill shook his head, pantomiming bewilderment— which, at the moment, came easily. Then he crouched in front of the nearest case and began, intently, to examine as ordinary a padlock as he could remember to have seen.

The window directly above him was, as he had noticed earlier, protected by venetian blinds, set to slant downward toward the deck. Bill looked up, quickly, at the window above him.

He saw eyes and part—not enough—of a face. Then he saw movement, and then nothing.

From the height of the eyes, from what he had been able to see of the face, the observer had been a man. The man had not wanted to be caught looking. Which, since the spectacle of a detective staring moodily at locked boxes might legitimately interest almost any-one, was worth considering. Bill Weigand considered it briefly and again looked up. This time he saw nothing between the slats of the blinds. He stood up, resisted the impulse to do a little carefree whistling, and sauntered—he could not resist that—to the near-est door off the deck. He stepped over the high sill, and turned right. The three staterooms which over-looked the boxes were P 19, P 21 and P 23.

The doors of the rooms were closed. The room from which the observer—almost certainly a man—had looked out was P 21. Bill knocked on it, expecting nothing. He got nothing. He turned the doorknob and found it locked. Bill walked aft through the starboard passageway. The other room from which the cases could be observed, although less easily, was P 25. He went down to A Deck and to the purser's office.

Stateroom P 21 was occupied by Mrs. and Miss Macklin. And Mr. and Mrs. Carl Buckley occupied P 19. The occupants of P 23 were named Conklin, which struck no note at all. But Respected Captain J. R. Folsom occupied, alone, stateroom P 25—from which he could have kept an angled eye on his arsenal.

Bill went aft to the sun deck, and found only a few sunning, the Norths and Dorian not among them. He went down to the promenade deck, and observed that Mr. and Mrs. Buckley were among the swimmers—and that Staff Captain Smythe-Hornsby was permit-ting himself an off-duty drink, in the company of Mr. Hammond Jones.

Bill found an unoccupied deck chair in the sun and paused to consider.

At a certain stage—Bill could remember very few cases in which this had not been true—a shape of things begins to form in the attentive mind. The shape is vague at first—amorphous at the center and, at the circumference, diffusing into mist. But the shape is there—the incipient shape. The task, thereafter, is one of definition. When the shape begins to appear, no little part of the job is done, although the hardest part may still remain.

But the circumstances which had led to the death of J. Orville Marsh, to the attack on young Cholly Pinkham, had, still, no semblance of a shape. Bill went back over it—went to Folsom's sudden appearance at a stateroom door; to the varied—and still incomprehensible—effects of the dead detective. He considered Mrs. Macklin's shrill, almost hysterical, assertion that someone had prowled her room—an assertion to which events of the past few minutes gave some confirmation. Someone, not Mrs. Macklin and not her daughter, had stood at the window of the room and peered out of it—and had got out of the room long before Bill reached the door. (Or, still in it, had merely waited for Bill to go away?) He tried to fit, with these things, the search of his own stateroom and the oddly half-hearted attack on Pam North. Bill smiled faintly to himself over the last. Since she had not been hurt, nor Jerry either, the occurrence had had its almost comic aspects. He sought to add to these things the presence on the *Carib Queen* of a polished young man who might once have involved himself in the theft of jewels, and he considered, also, the apparent determination of a physically attractive young woman to put her worst foot forward.

And no shape appeared. One could not, as Pam had previously pointed out, add apples and elephants. There was no shape—and there was no glaring absence of shape. Distortion may mean as much as conformity; the just perceptibly erratic behavior of an orbit-following celestial body may hint at the presence of another body previously unseen and lead to a search for it. . . . It was proving easy to grow drowsy in the sun. And then something in Bill's mind said, "Wait." Obediently, Bill waited. A glimmer came to him.

About the murder itself there had been a kind of preposterousness. It was as if a prank had been played—an absurd, unlikely prank—and had got out of hand. There was something outrageous about it, and something incongruous. That the sword had been sharpened to cut a wedding cake in Worcester, Massachusetts, was somehow the final touch.

But the attack on Pinkham had been, in method and execution, as unlike the murder of Marsh as one act of violence can easily be unlike another. On the young steward, a blackjack had been used—from the nature of the wound, that was almost certain. And a blackjack is as professional as a sawed-off shotgun. Bill had been a policeman too long, encountered too many of the vagaries of crime, to believe that a murderer always limits himself to one weapon. But a sword and a blackjack—and then, with Pam North, the mere laying on of heavy hands. Variety was being carried to extremes.

Bill considered this distortion. It occurred to him that the distortion might have been provided for that very purpose—the confusion of a diligent detective. It was, of course, also conceivable that several things were going on at the same time—which would be disorderly of them, but not unprecedented.

It was, Bill thought, all very disorderly. The atmosphere of a pleasure cruise and a murder investigation fitted as badly together as a sword and a blackjack. Embarked on such a cruise, people leave their backgrounds behind them. But a crime is like an iceberg, floating for the most part submerged—the iceberg in its ocean, the crime in its past.

He left the sunny chair and went forward, stopping at the purser's bureau. There he made a request that Mr. Jules Barron be paged and, on his response, asked to attend the captain in his cabin. Bill then walked forward, to inform Captain Cunningham of a visitor to be expected. He went through the smoke room on his way.

Respected Captain J. R. Folsom and Mrs. Macklin were together at a table, with drinks in front of them. Folsom appeared to be doing most of the talking. On the other hand, Mrs. Macklin seemed to be doing most of the drinking. Folsom had an untouched glass in front of him. Hers was almost empty.

The Norths were, rather uncharacteristically, drinking tea. It had been Pam who suggested it, after they had, by mutual consent, left the movie at its middle. They might, she said, as well find out what went on "up there." Up there was the Grand Lounge, which was across the Grand Entrance from the smoke room as one went forward on the sun deck of the *Carib Queen*. In the Grand Lounge dwelt dignity, and what was going on was tea.

The lounge was a large room, stretching the width of the ship, with wide windows on three sides. Its frequenters turned out to be somewhat older, on the average, than those of the smoke room, although a younger group clustered at a piano and told each other to play "that" and then sang to "that," but in moderate voices. Elsewhere bridge went on, and canasta and the serving of tea. The Norths had tea and small, neat sandwiches, and looked through a window at the sparkling south Atlantic. Or was it already the Caribbean, or even the Gulf of Mexico? "They ought to mark them," Pam said, and poured more tea, which really they ought to drink oftener. The idea of labeling such large bodies of water engaged them both, and they proposed methods—Pam had an idea that it might somehow be done with kites, at least in pleasant weather. It was agreeable, for once, to have nothing to do except label oceans.

But the public-address system, although its tone was dulcet, brought them back. It requested that Mr. Jules Barron communicate with the purser. And it was at precisely that moment that Pam, looking around the pleasant room at the pleasant people, found that three of the people were Mr. and Mrs. Furstenberg and Hilda Macklin.

They were at a table, across the room from the Norths, and teacups were in front of them—and Hilda was leaning a little forward, talking with what seemed, as seen from a distance, to be marked concentration. Furstenberg listened to her gravely, and shook his head—but whether in negation, or perhaps in sympathy, was only to be guessed. There was an expression of gravity, also on Mrs. Furstenberg's cheerful face.

"Will Mr. Jules Barron please communicate with the purser?" the public-address system asked, for the second time. And then it seemed to Pam, still watching the three—the perhaps rather oddly assorted three?— that the repetition of the request interrupted Hilda Macklin, and that she broke off, as if in mid-sentence, and raised her head as if listening. And this, if true, was somewhat interesting.

And then, from the group around the piano, a good-looking—an almost dashing—dark young man detached himself and began to walk through the room toward the door.

It was, Pam realized, the same dark young man who had—perhaps—made some slight efforts to strike up an acquaintance with Hilda Macklin, and had seemed to get nowhere.

If it was also Mr. Jules Barron, on his way to communicate with the purser, it would be—perhaps—quite interesting, although precisely why it should be was not immediately apparent, even to Pam herself.

If Bill hadn't left them out of the party in the captain's quarters before lunch, she wouldn't have to wonder if the man was Jules Barron. For that exclusion, Bill almost deserved not to be told that at the mention of Barron's name Hilda had—perhaps—broken off what she was saying and made a gesture of sudden attention, even of surprise. Almost deserved—but, of course, not quite.

8

Apparently Mr. Jules Barron had assumed his summons was to another party. He did not say so. But, finding only Captain Cunningham and Weigand in the captain's quarters, he permitted dark eyebrows to rise in polite enquiry. He was told, by Captain Cunningham, that it was good of him to come. Cunningham then looked at Weigand and waited.

"We have a problem, Mr. Barron," Bill said. "We think you may be able to help us."

"Me?" Barron said, and then added that he doubted it, but that, of course, anything he could do.

"Right," Bill said. "The problem we have concerns a murder. A man named Marsh has been killed."

This time, Barron's eyebrows indicated astonishment.

"On the boat?" he asked, and Cunningham winced slightly, and Bill said, "Right, Mr. Barron. Mr. Marsh was a private detective." To this, Jules Barron, who was gayly arrayed, said he didn't get it. He looked from one to another, and repeated that he didn't get it. "Why me?" he asked, amplifying.

"The photographs of jewelry," Bill said. "The ones

we were looking at earlier. Mr. Marsh had them in his possession when he was killed."

Then, Barron's eyes narrowed, just perceptibly.

"Your wife's great-aunt," he said, to Captain Cunningham. "So that was a lot of baloney. You know, it sounded like baloney."

He looked at Weigand, then.

"So," he said, "what's it got to do with me?"

But his eyes were wary, and it was evident he could guess. He sat down.

"I think," Bill told him, "you had seen those photographs before, Mr. Barron. Or—the things themselves. You were anxious to get your hands on them. And, when you did, all you needed was a quick glance."

"All right," Barron said. "That's what you think. So that's what you think."

"It isn't true?"

Weigand was damn' right, it wasn't true. The varnish came off Barron's speech. Cops could make mistakes. It wouldn't be the first time—He stopped.

"No," Bill said. "Not the first time, is it?"

"Oh, I get it," Barron said. "I get it all right. Because there was this little mix-up about an old dame who couldn't remember where she put her pretties—" He broke off again, with a rather elaborate shrug. "Nobody charged me with anything. They wanted a fall-guy and tried me for size. And, I didn't fit. So they said, 'Sorry, please'—only they didn't, you can bet on that. All they said was 'Scram!' So now you come along."

He stood up. He displayed indignation, presumably righteous. He spoke to Captain Cunningham, and got some of the varnish on again. He said that if that was all it was—

"No," Bill said. "Sit down, Mr. Barron."

"You," Barron said, "are off your beat, aren't you?"

He looked hard at Bill Weigand, then at the captain. He was looked back at, harder.

"You can take it, Mr. Barron," Cunningham said, "that Captain Weigand has got himself a new beat. As he said, sit down."

And Jules Barron sat down, which came as rather a surprise to Captain Cunningham, and interested Bill Weigand not a little, since he was off his beat and since Cunningham's authority, while considerable, did not really extend to the forcible detention of passengers. It appeared that Barron had had a change of mind, and a rather sudden one.

"This woman who lost her jewelry," Bill said. "What was her name, by the way?"

"Morgan," Barron said. "Believe it or not. And I was clean on it. Couldn't have been cleaner."

"She got it back?" Bill said.

Barron said, "Yeah. She got it back."

He paused a moment, and spoke quickly.

"That's the way I heard it," he said. "I didn't know a damn' thing about it. Not about any of it."

"Through a contact?" Bill asked him.

"I wouldn't know."

"Possibly," Bill said, "through a private detective? Working with the thieves and with the agency—both sides of the street?"

"I wouldn't know."

"You've heard of that being done?"

"Sure," Barron said. "I've heard of it. Who hasn't?"

"Mr. Barron," Bill said, "did you know Mr. Marsh? Was he involved in this—mix-up?"

"Never heard of him," Barron said. "As to whether he was in the Morgan deal—that is, helped get back Mrs. Morgan's stuff—how would I know? I don't know a damn' thing, like I told you."

And then, suddenly, Barron, who had been looking at nothing in particular while he spoke, looked up at Bill Weigand—and smiled. There was in the smile precisely what Bill least wanted to see—confidence. But there had been a moment—the moment when Barron had been stared down, failed, as he might have, to walk out of the captain's quarters—when Bill had thought Jules Barron was not confident at all.

The answer was as easy to guess as it was discouraging to contemplate—if, in relation to Jules Barron, there was a track to get on, Bill had got off it.

"To get back to the jewelry in the photographs," Bill said. "Had you ever seen it before?"

"No," Barron said.

"Not the photographs? Nor the things themselves— a bracelet, two necklaces, a diamond ring?"

"No."

"You did want to look at them?"

"Everybody else was," Barron told him. "I'm as curious as the next guy." He looked at Captain Cunningham. "Quite a story about this great-aunt," he said. "Quite a story." He paused. He looked at Bill Weigand and his gaze was shrewd. "All for my benefit?" he asked.

He was not directly answered.

"How did you happen to come on this cruise?" Bill asked him, and was merely casting at random, and hoped it was not too evident.

Barron's eyebrows, which had been at rest, went up.

"Why does anybody?" he said. "Read about it. Thought it might be fun. Had a little loose cash."

"Didn't know anybody who was going to take the trip?"

"I tell you," Barron said, "the way I see it, you always meet people. New faces. See what I mean?"

"Elderly women with money?" Bill asked him.

Barron did not look angry. He merely looked amused.

"Is there a law against it?" he asked, as man of the world to man of the world.

He was told he could go. He went smiling, and the smile was confident.

"A rather unpleasant young man," Captain Cunningham said. "But—"

"Right," Bill said. "He'd seen the jewelry before— the pictures or the real thing. But as you say—but." He lighted a cigarette and looked at it. "Didn't ask the right questions," he said. "I'm afraid it comes to that."

"But there are right questions?"

Bill shrugged. He said he hoped so, that he thought so.

"Usually," Captain Cunningham said. "Usually, on trips like this, there'll be several middle-aged women traveling by themselves. Widows, y'know—children grown up. That sort of thing. Pretty much at loose ends, the old gals are. Not rolling in it, or they take world cruises. But not hard up by a long shot—and lonely. My grandmother's day, they'd have settled down to it—tea with the vicar. That sort of thing. Some of these haven't, if you take me."

Bill nodded his head. He took the captain without difficulty.

"Brings men of Barron's type, y'know," the captain said. "Bound to, I'm afraid. Could be that's all there is to it, eh? Might account for Barron's getting the wind up, you think?"

The trouble was, Bill pointed out, that Barron hadn't got the wind up—or, if he had momentarily, had quickly got it down again. But the captain's theory might account for Barron.

"One trouble is," Bill said, "we may be looking at the wrong group entirely. Under normal circumstances, we pretty much know our group—that much, anyway. Here—" He spread his hands. "There are no sure relationships," he said. "We're merely all in the same boat."

"Makes it difficult," Captain Cunningham agreed. From the adjoining room, which apparently served as pantry, there was the sound of dishes being moved. "Like to have you stay," Cunningham said, taking care of that. "All new faces, this round."

Bill looked at his watch, found it was a few minutes after six. He did not stay.

They sat at a table for four on the verge of the dance floor in the Coral Café, and it was a little after ten on Sunday evening—twelve hours or so out of Havana. Pam wore a short dinner dress of the palest yellow; Dorian was in a longer one of white, high in front and by no means high behind. An entertainer—female, under an amber spot near the piano—entertained with imitations. She finished, or at any rate paused, and the master of ceremonies urged a great big hand. The hand was of medium size. They didn't know, the master of ceremonies told them, as the hand subsided, how much talent they had among them—right among the passengers. He wanted to ask a man they all knew to take a bow. Just wait until they heard his name—Al Brighton. Al *Brighton! Whoops!*

Jerry North looked at Bill Weigand. Dorian looked at Pam.

"Whoops indeed," Pam said, and the sound of her voice was covered by another moderate hand. "Wait a minute—he writes a column or something. For a tabloid or something. Wait—it's all full of *poetry*. About being ourselves and how little little children are and the scent of new mown hay. And mothers, of course."

"Not that one!" Dorian said, but it was—with tousled hair, homespun in spite of a midnight-blue dinner jacket and a checkered cummerbund. Mr. Brighton not only took a bow. Pressed, lightly, he recited. The one he recited was not about mother; it was about dear old sis, who brought us up by hand.

"Dickens," Jerry said, absently. *"Great Expectations,* as I remember it. He must have seen the movie."

But nothing can disturb, too deeply, on a cruise from fall to summer, with a bright moon moving gently up and down beyond windows as a ship moves; with the cool warmth of sea air finding its way in through french doors which open on a deck which has become a moon deck. As all things pass, Mr. Brighton passed. (After an encore, about the desirability of playing the game, come what might.) The orchestra started up again, and couples drifted to the dance floor and Pam said, indicating with her head, "There. Is that Mr. Barron?"

It was.

"Then," Pam said, "she does. As I told you."

Explanation was not required. It had been given over pre-dinner cocktails in the smoke room. The name of Jules Barron meant enough to Hilda Macklin for her to interrupt what she was saying, and make a quick, almost startled, movement of her head. And the same Jules Barron was the handsome, the really dashing, dark young man who had attempted—or might have attempted—to strike up an acquaintance with Mrs. Macklin's slender daughter, who had so much more than she gave herself credit for.

It was something which Bill could have borne to have known earlier. He had said so at cocktails; now that Barron's identity was confirmed, he said so again.

"If you will leave us out of things," Pam said, and she had said that before.

"You're fairly sure he did try to—strike up an acquaintance?" Bill asked. "Or—were they already acquainted, but not advertising it?"

"Either way," Pam said. "But I'm only fairly sure. Of course, he's not her type at all. Or the other way around, when you come to that. Although if that mother of hers would only let her get some decent clothes—"

"It would have given you something, if you'd known sooner?" Jerry asked, when Pam did not bother to finish the obvious.

It would have given him another question to ask, Bill said. Another answer to listen to. He was not sure that anything else would have come of it, or would come of it now.

Hilda Macklin and her mother came into the café from the deck outside. Mrs. Macklin, in metallic blue, seemed quite sober. Hilda wore a straight white dress, high at the neck. She just won't do *anything,* Pam thought, and wished she knew Hilda Macklin well enough to shake her. At least, she might wear lipstick. Hilda sat beside her mother on a banquette, at one of the less desirable tables. Clearly—far too clearly—

they had come to watch the dancing. Mrs. Macklin was, quickly, served with what appeared to be a double brandy in a snifter. Hilda had a small glass of what, probably, was sherry.

Jerry stood up and held a hand down to Pam who said, "Why, Jerry. Without urging?" and stood up and they went onto the dance floor. There was little movement in the ship now, or she had got used to it. At any rate, the dance floor did not seem quite so hilly as it had before.

Bill Weigand, example set, half stood at the table, and then sat down again. Respected Captain Folsom, in uniform but with a black bow tie for formality, came to the table and asked Bill if he had a minute. Invited, he sat.

"Mrs. North tell you what I told her?" Folsom asked and, as he looked at Bill and waited, his gray eyes seemed shrewd—at variance, somehow, with the portly ruddiness which was the outward semblance of J. R. Folsom. "About the woman he was looking for? Marsh, I mean?"

"Yes," Bill said.

"I was talking to this Mrs. Macklin earlier," Folsom said. "The one with prowlers in her cabin? Red-haired lady?"

"Yes," Bill said.

"Knows Boston," Folsom said. "I made a point of finding out. Says she never lived there but I gave, you know, one or two false steers. About streets and things like that. Straightened me out. She knows Boston. Well?"

"Apparently," Bill said, "the woman he was trying to locate has been located. In California."

"Apparently?" Folsom repeated, and his eyes narrowed.

"Her family says so," Bill told him. "Her daughter and her son. And—she only has one daughter."

"All the same," Folsom said, "Mrs. Macklin knows Boston and lets on she doesn't. Funny color hair she's got."

"Yes," Bill said. "I gather you're trying to give me a hand, Mr. Folsom? Figure I need one?"

"The way I figure it," Folsom said, "somebody used our sword. And—I showed up at the wrong time."

"So you play detective," Bill said.

He was told he could call it that. He was asked who was to stop it.

"Search for clues? In other people's staterooms?"

Bill was looked at with noticeable blankness. He was told Folsom had no idea what he was talking about.

"Right," Bill said. "Not a good idea, Mr. Folsom. And—while you're here, I'd like to show you something."

He reached into a pocket of his jacket and took out the letter, on Clover Club stationery, which some indecipherable person had addressed to J. Orville Marsh. He folded the letter so that only the intricate signature showed, and held it for Folsom to see, but not to take. Folsom looked at it, and Bill Weigand looked at him.

For a second, Bill thought, Folsom's shrewd gray eyes went blank. But it was only for a second—not even for a second. Then Folsom looked at Bill, and there was nothing to be read in his eyes.

"You don't recognize it?" Bill asked him, and Folsom, after continuing for an instant to look at Bill, shook his head. Then he said, "Why?" and his voice was hard on the word.

"A member of the Clover Club in Worcester, apparently," Bill said, and put the letter back into his pocket. "You are too, aren't you?"

"Checking on me?" Folsom said.

"Among others," Bill told him.

"Then you know," Folsom said, and stood up. "I'm not your man," he said, and looked down.

"Right," Bill said, pleasantly, and Folsom looked at him again, and shook his head, and went away.

"Such a gay evening," Dorian said, and got her hand patted, and was told she knew what she had married—had known it a long time.

"Oh," she said, "I ask no change. Shall we da—" The music stopped. "Damn," Dorian said, simply. And then she said, "Look who's here, now."

It is to be assumed that the master of a ship has the run of it. It was, however, a privilege of which Captain Peter Cunningham, RNR, had not before much availed himself, being content to appear at his table and to mingle otherwise only with those invited to his quarters. (Pam had wondered whether he really liked sherry as much as he seemed to, and had been asked whether she wanted a ship's captain to train on whisky. She had responded that it was one of Jerry's theories that he drove better after a couple of drinks, and that a ship was probably much the same—larger, but encountering less traffic.) Now Captain Cunningham, looking as distinguished as a man may, in a white mess jacket, had invaded the Coral Café.

He had just arrived, and he was being affable, as one to the practice born. He had, perhaps by intention, timed his arrival with the orchestra's break, but he seemed otherwise to have no plan—to be merely, in line of duty, adding his cachet to the gathering. He paused at this table and that, and sat briefly at one or two, although he, it appeared, refused drinks at all. He was a more elegant, entirely non-fluttering, Miss Springer; and Bill Weigand, after a moment of puzzlement, watched him with growing amusement. Captain Cunningham, although in the main anything but an ingenuous man, was a little obviously putting on an act.

Captain Cunningham greeted the Norths, who, with no music to dance to, were bound toward the deck outside. He paused briefly at the table occupied by Mrs. Macklin and her daughter; momentarily, he joined a small knot of Respectable Riflemen. And very gradually, Bill Weigand decided, the captain was making his way in the direction of the Weigands' table. He reached it just as the orchestra reassembled. Bill stood up, in deference to authority. The captain sat down. He hoped they were enjoying the entertainment—he'd been told the impersonations were really quite good. "If one likes that sort of thing," he added, doubtfully. Invited, he said he might break down and have a sherry. "Don't like the stuff particularly," he said, somewhat absently. "But there you are. Discretion, y'know."

"Quite," Dorian said, and sipped brandy.

"As a matter of fact," Captain Cunningham said, to Bill, "I was rather looking for you. You too, of course." The last was to Dorian. "Looking particularly nice tonight, if you don't mind my saying so."

Dorian did not mind. She was glad he thought so.

"It's all over the ship," Cunningham said, then. "And—they seem to be getting the straight of it, or thereabouts. About Marsh, I mean."

"It was always only a matter of time," Bill told him. "Someone specifically?"

"Yes," Cunningham said. "Our friend Furstenberg.

Thought you'd want to hear about it, but didn't want to make a point of it. So I came here. Accidental meeting, y'know. Can't say I come often." He paused. "Entertainers," he said, explaining all. "Well, about our friend Furstenberg—"

Immediately after dinner, Aaron Furstenberg had asked if he might have a word with the captain, and had been taken to the captain's quarters to have it. He had come, unhurriedly but directly enough, to his point, which he said he thought possibly a curious one. But first—was what was rumored true? That something had happened to Mr. Marsh? He was told it was, and told, briefly, what had happened, and had moved his elderly, dignified head slowly up and down, as if confirming something in his own mind. He had one other question—was the jewelry of which the captain had such excellent photographs, in any way connected with the unfortunate thing that had happened to Mr. Marsh?

Captain Cunningham had hesitated over that. Finally he had said, "Why?"

Furstenberg slowly moved his head again, as if Captain Cunningham had said "Yes." "Suppose I had, or near enough," the captain said, telling it to Bill Weigand.

He asked, Furstenberg said, because he had, only a little time before, remembered having heard of Marsh, and of Marsh in connection with precious stones. The memory dated back some years; it had to do with the retention of Marsh by a firm of jewelers with which Furstenberg had been connected. "It had nothing to do with me," Furstenberg said. "I know none of the details, although as I recall it concerned a trusted employee and—some question of appraisal." He did remember that it had all been handled very carefully, and that nothing had come of it—nothing, at any rate, which involved publicity. Captain Cunningham would appreciate what he meant.

"Felt he knew more about whatever it was than he wanted to let out," Cunningham said, to Bill Weigand. "Being discreet, if you follow me." Bill nodded.

But it had not really been his recollection of this incident which had brought Furstenberg to the captain. At least—Aaron Furstenberg sought precision—not primarily that. But it had occurred to him that the photographs of the various articles—quite valuable articles, insofar as one could tell from photographs—might be somehow related to Marsh. Should he, now, proceed on that assumption?

Captain Cunningham gave him permission.

Then—Miss Hilda Macklin had come to Furstenberg that afternoon. "One of the ladies at the table," Furstenberg said, in case it might have slipped the captain's mind. "The pale young lady?" Captain Cunningham admitted recognition of Miss Hilda Macklin.

"Mrs. Furstenberg and I were having tea," Furstenberg said. "Very excellent tea, by the way. Miss Macklin came to our table, apologized for bothering us, and wondered if I could give her some advice. Naturally, I asked her to join us."

She had joined them. She had understood that he was a man who knew much about precious stones. She was—it was embarrassing to come, in this way, to a stranger. To impose. But—

She wanted advice about selling some jewelry—some quite old pieces which had been long in the family. But—

"She seemed," Furstenberg said, "to be very embarrassed indeed. We both felt quite sorry for her."

The jewelry was her mother's. Her mother—well, to

be honest, they were running short of money. There had always seemed to be—so much. When she was a child she had thought that—well, she had never really thought about it. But that wasn't what she wanted to say. That didn't, really, have anything to do with it. Although, she supposed, in another way it had everything. There were, then, these several pieces which, she thought, must have considerable value. But—she felt so helpless, so in need of advice. Seeing Mr. Furstenberg sitting there she had—It had been an impulse.

It was not, she had said, as if the things—a bracelet, a diamond bracelet, in particular—were things her mother would now have occasion to wear. They were—"the kind of pieces one wears to big events. Like to the opera." As for herself, she would never go any place where one wore such lovely things. And, even if this had not been true, they needed money. She had only recently discovered how much they needed money. If she had known even a few weeks ago, they would never have spent "all this" money on the cruise. But her mother had no sense of money. No sense at all about it.

"She seemed very upset," Furstenberg said, telling Captain Cunningham about it. "Her mother does seem a little odd and—Miss Macklin is very young, of course. With little experience. Apparently, she hoped that I would buy the pieces. I had to explain that I was retired and that I had never, in the way she apparently meant, dealt in precious stones."

Then, if he would not buy the pieces, would he advise? Specifically, wasn't there someone in Havana he could tell her about? Some dealer she could trust? Because, knowing so little, she would have no way of telling whether an offer was—reasonable. She had paused, then, and put her hands to her head, as if in distress.

"We have to get some money right away," she said. "It's—it's dreadfully urgent."

Furstenberg had been solicitous, had tried to calm her, because he felt that she was growing increasingly excited and upset. He had asked for more detail about the pieces, and had been told there was the diamond bracelet, "all diamonds"—and several other things, and a pearl necklace. She had always thought the bracelet was very valuable.

"I urged her to wait until she got back to New York," Furstenberg said. "To have the articles appraised by some reliable man—not to trust to a shipboard acquaintance. I pointed out that I, for example, might for all she knew be entirely unscrupulous. That I might, for example, send her to a dishonest dealer in Havana and—have an arrangement with him. She said, 'No. I can tell.' So many people imagine they can. They are often wrong. But—finally, I gave her the name of a firm in Havana. An entirely reliable firm, although I imagine she could do better in New York."

He had stopped, then. He had said that that was all he had wanted to tell the captain. But he had looked at the captain carefully, as if he expected comment.

"Bracelets such as she described aren't too common, I imagine," Cunningham told him, and Furstenberg appeared to have got what he expected. At any rate, he said, "Precisely, captain," and then took his dignified way out of the captain's quarters. After thinking it over, Captain Cunningham had taken his own way out of them, and found Bill Weigand. Unobtrusively. He sipped his sherry, at the table on the edge of the dance floor, in the Coral Café.

"He puts two and two together," Bill said. "Comes up with—stolen jewels, I suppose. And with Marsh trying to recover them and getting killed for his pains. And, a desire to unload them fast."

"You don't like it?" Cunningham said.

"It would," Bill told him, "be pleasantly simple. And—a pleasantly simple thief, if Miss Macklin is one. Asking a stranger to name a good reliable fence."

Captain Cunningham said, "Quite." Then he said, "Perhaps the old girl has been having her on?"

Anything, Bill supposed, was possible. But one would think the young girl would know if "old family pieces" weren't.

"Did she offer to show them to Furstenberg?"

"He didn't say so," Cunningham told him. "I gathered—well, that he wanted to stay out of it as much as possible. When he began to think there was a smell of fish. Can't blame him, y'know."

Bill agreed one could not blame Aaron Furstenberg, assuming all was as he said it was. Cunningham raised eyebrows.

"Oh," Bill said, "probably it was."

"One thing," Captain Cunningham said, "once you've bought your ticket on a do like this, the need for cash isn't pressing. Drinks, of course. Run to a bit with Mrs. Macklin. And the things women buy ashore. And tips. But, it isn't as if they risked being stranded."

"Right," Bill said. "I'd thought of that."

Cunningham supposed he had. Cunningham said he would be getting along, then. He got along, stopping to smile and speak, but progressing consistently toward a door. The orchestra reappeared. The captain's pace quickened.

Bill looked at Dorian, and found her sketching on

the back of the drink menu. He was not surprised—a pencil seemed, sometimes, to grow in Dorian's hand. She held the sketch so that he could see it.

It was a head of Mrs. Macklin—a head, and a hand holding glass to lips, but not so that the face was obscured. It was done, as were most of Dorian Weigand's sketches, in few lines—it intimated, rather than described, a face. It was evidently Mrs. Macklin. It was also all women like Mrs. Macklin. At the same time, there was something unreal about the face.

"It does odd things to faces, doesn't it?" Dorian said, as Bill studied the face of Mrs. Macklin. "Pulls them out of shape—so that they're not right for the bones."

Without, for the moment, entirely understanding what she said, he saw, clearly enough, what she meant. He said, "What does?" and Dorian said, "Oh, lifting, of course. Surely you'd seen that?"

9

The after portion of the sun deck, off which the café opened, from which one could look down on the swimming pool, was lighted by the soft glow of night. The moon gave light, the stars added a little light, light trickled through doors and windows of the café. The ship itself steamed to the south, and now to the west, in an effulgence of its own, in which the sun deck shared. But there was, certainly, nothing garish in the illumination of the deck, now that night covered it. The cruise brochure had spoken, warmly, of the romance of tropical nights, and it could not be denied that the brochure had something. Neither the Norths nor the Weigands sought to deny it. On the softly lighted deck, in the night's warmth, it was difficult to keep one's mind on murder, and no great effort was made.

They sat relaxed in deck chairs, in a row near the rail. They sipped, less from thirst than in obeisance to the spirit of holiday. Through open doors and windows of the café the orchestra's music filtered, and it sounded much better from this little distance. The girl entertainer was singing, now, and to her efforts, also, distance lent a modicum of enchantment. Around them, but not too near, other shadowed figures were dim in other deck chairs, and now and then there were muted voices, and now and then a woman laughed, but softly, in accordance with the theme.

Pam and Jerry had come out from dancing and found the Weigands in repose, and had joined them in repose—at least until the entertainer finished. A steward had brought them drinks. "All we need is fireflies," Pam said, but here and there a cigarette glowed in the dimness, which was almost as good. "We'll bring them, another time," Jerry said, beside her, and it did not seem preposterous—on such a night, in such a place, there could be nothing preposterous and nothing harsh.

The orchestra quit playing, and there were only low voices and, pervasively, the sound of water moving about the little ship, headed now toward the island of Cuba. Pam wished, idly, that she could think of a few appropriate lines of poetry, but found she could not, and abandoned the effort in midstream—let it drift away on the stream, as all else seemed to drift. She was half asleep, and Jerry was more than half, when the music commenced again.

"One more," Jerry said, and stood up, and Pam was too relaxed, too accepting, to be more than slightly astonished at this improbable Gerald North, who usually had to be led—perhaps dragged was the more precise word—to the dance. She aroused herself and stood up, and they looked down at the Weigands. "The effort," Dorian said, "would be great, as Mr. Porter once said of sloths. In another connection."

The Norths went off toward the café, seeming to float. "Unless you want to?" Dorian said to Bill, who said, dreamily, "Mmm." Tired by this exertion, they relaxed. Bill, to prove companionship—but to prove nothing—reached out and took her hand. Her slim fingers curled around his hand. It was some minutes before he realized that her fingers were cold; it was somewhat longer before he associated this fact with the corresponding fact that, on the sun deck, it was no longer as warm as it had been. "You're cold," he told her, without accusation. "Shall we go inside?"

"Not yet," she said. "It's too perfect. Am I cold?"

"You feel cold," Bill said. He ran fingers up her bare, brown arm. "You feel quite cold."

"To be practical," Dorian said, "I have very little on. Perhaps I am a little chilly. I suppose I should have brought something out. But, it's too nice here."

He would, Bill said, get her something. The yellow thing? She smiled at him. She thought, as Pam had thought before, that the atmosphere of a cruise brought out something in husbands. It was pleasant that it did. "If you like," she said. "The yellow thing, by all means." He would not be a minute, Bill told her, and—after some seconds spent in pulling himself together—rose with resolution from the deck chair and went about it. And, left alone, Dorian discovered that she was, really, rather too chilly for comfort. While she waited for the yellow thing, to be brought for her naked back by this charmingly attentive man, she would stir around.

She stirred. She walked a little way forward, and then a little way aft, among chairs which, now, for the most part were empty. It must, she thought, be late. It would have been more sensible to go in, even to go to the cabin, where it would be warm enough—into which they would carry their private warmth. When Bill came back—

She stood at the low rail which, amidship, was curved in to conform to the shape of the swimming pool below, so that, standing by it, one could look down on swimmers. But in the daytime, not at night. At night the pool was drained and cleaned, and left empty until morning.

She looked aft over the ship's stern and was entranced. Water, water which seemed to froth in its own light, boiled from beneath the ship, white against the darkness of the other water. It was like a waterfall foaming upward—a water *rise,* she thought. There was a kind of phosphorescence about the violent white water. And, watching it, one felt that the ship, pushing the water behind it, was plunging into the night, where before the ship had seemed to float motionless.

Far behind the ship, fading slowly into the darkness, the whiteness of the wake stretched—stretched straight into distance. It ended in the darkness, but that was only because of the darkness. If it were light, she thought—chose to think—one could look to the limit of one's vision and see the white path the ship had taken, stretching to, stretching beyond, the horizon.

She had her hands lightly on the rail, leaned forward a little so that she might better see the dancing of white water. She heard steps behind her and started to turn toward Bill, and in the same instant knew the steps were wrong, not his, and then, still with no time to move, felt a violent impact on her back, struggled to regain balance and knew herself falling. As she fell, she cried out. And, as she fell, she twisted herself, as a diver twists—as a cat twists—instinctively to control her fall.

Bill saw her fall. He had, climbing from A Deck, gone to the promenade deck and along it toward one of the steep flights which, outside the ship's enclosure, led from the promenade deck and the pool area, to the deck above. He saw her, a swirl of white, falling toward the pool, and heard her cry out. And ran—

Dorian, twisting as she fell, fell some ten feet. She landed on her back. She landed on the protective netting which, each night, was rigged above the empty pool. She lay still on the tight-stretched netting.

Bill ran toward her, and at the same time others ran—from the café on the deck above, from chairs on the promenade deck. A deck steward plunged down the stairway from the sun deck and, from somewhere, there was the violent, high sound of a boatswain's whistle, and after that more men ran.

Bill reached her first. She turned her head toward him and her eyes were open.

"Knocked—breath—out," Dorian Weigand said, in a voice that proved it. "Somebody—pushed—"

He reached toward her, working his way out on the netting until he could reach her. She rolled, then, to hands and knees and when he said, "Wait!" said, in much her ordinary voice, "Oh, I'm all right."

And she was, or nearly. Her unprotected back was welted by the rope and, she assured him, the dress, lower down, had been of insufficient protection. He would find, she said, clinging to him, that she looked like a waffle iron. But—she was all right.

That the ship's surgeon confirmed, and that she was extraordinarily lucky to be all right. Falling face down to a rope netting, with the chance of being tangled and twisted in it—that might have been very unlucky indeed.

"Luck nothing," Dorian said, allowed to go with Bill to their stateroom. "I wiggled around."

She did not, Bill agreed, move like a cat for nothing.

He was still white from the shock of her fall; was, he decided, the shakier of the two.

But he, as he saw her fall, had forgotten the netting which would save her from a plunge to the steel bottom of the empty pool, and to death or cruel injury on it.

Someone else had forgotten it too. That, as Dorian told what little she had to tell—told of footsteps behind her; of the sudden forceful push against her back— became evident.

"Why me?" Dorian said, turning over to lie on her stomach. "What have I done to anybody?"

There was, then, no answer. It was only apparent that, with murder in mind, someone had moved out of the shadows of the dimly lit deck, moved softly until the last and then with a rush, indifferent to sound, and had pushed Dorian Weigand into what the attacker had supposed would be an empty swimming pool, its bottom twenty feet below the rail.

The ship's surgeon had provided two yellow capsules, and instructions—instructions which, Bill insisted, should be followed. A compromise was reached; she took one. After a time she slept, at first, restlessly, turning often in search of comfort, but then more quietly. Bill, in his bed across the stateroom, watched until finally she was quiet. He left a dim light burning so that he could watch her, moment by moment reassure himself. But he did not know what he watched against.

When she slept deeply, he began to fan his mind, seeking to stir that spark which might, nurtured, turn into a light. More things had happened, but they added only confusion. The attack on Dorian—to that there was no answer. An attack, as if by proxy, on him? But why? He could not, gloomily, see that at the moment he threatened anyone. The threads were tangled, and he did not progress in their untangling. A red thread, a green thread. Like electric lead wires, colored for identification, like— Why, he wondered, as thought grew dim in sleep, did he think of two threads, two wires, tangled together. A spark almost glowed, but sleep doused it.

Things were much brighter in the morning, except in the minds of Bill and Dorian, Pam and Jerry North. The Caribbean was very bright; the ship shone in sunlight, and after a time there was land, at first low and dark and ahead, then—very quickly—off the port-side, and the land was Cuba. They would, their dining room steward told them, dock before noon. They breakfasted; Dorian insisted that she was as good as new, and looked it. But she did, Bill told them, look rather waffle-molded from behind. And there was a rope burn, just visible, on one brown arm. But she was as good as new, and with coffee better.

Bill left them after breakfast. They went to the sun deck, and stood at the rail—now and then looking over their shoulders, gripping the rail firmly—and down into the sparkling pool in which, already, some ca-vorted. The sun deck was very different now, with the sun on it. There were no shadows. The deck chairs, which at nights were huddled, were rearranged for day. Right here she had been standing, Dorian said, showing them. (The wake now was a churning sparkle in darker water, no longer frothing magic.) And she still could not be sure whether the footsteps heard so briefly behind her had been those of a man or of a woman.

"A man," Pam thought, and said. "The same one who pushed me, probably. A very pushing man."

They sat in chairs, and Dorian assured them that it

did not hurt a bit, although she did not sit, as she usually sat, in contained quiet. And they asked one another why, and came up with no very convincing answers.

Bill found Aaron Furstenberg, and got a name. He telephoned ahead to Havana, and got police headquarters, and identified himself through politely unwinding channels until he got to a man who had once been an opposite number. Bill explained. The one-time opposite number was co-operative. Matters would be expedited. Indeed, a car would be waiting. As to the other, assuredly. A man would watch. "The stake-out," the opposite number said, with no accent at all. But of the firm itself, they had only reports.

Bill telephoned again, after allowing ten minutes, during which he fanned his mind once more. The police had, indeed, communicated with Carrillo et Cie. by the time Bill got them on the telephone. Carrillo et Cie. did, indeed, know Señor Aaron Furstenberg, an expert of distinction. And the police had told them what was requested—if the señora came, they would examine, they would appraise. But they would not buy. It was understood.

Why Dorian? The question repeated itself in Bill's mind, and remained unanswered. He went forward from the telephone exchange on A Deck and up to the promenade deck, and knocked on the door of stateroom P 21. This time he was answered, rather piercingly. "Come in and get them," Mrs. Macklin said. "Took you long enough."

Bill opened the door and was looked at. Mrs. Macklin was fully dressed, in a suit of purplish complexion. She was sitting in a chair behind a table on which were breakfast dishes. She held in one hand—a thin hand in which the tendons showed—a glass of what, one might presume, was tomato juice, at any rate basically. She looked at Weigand through piercing black eyes and told him he wasn't the boy.

"Thought you were the boy," she said. "Come for these." She indicated the dishes. "Well?" He started to speak. "Understand this Marsh man is dead," she said. "Dead while I was looking all over the ship for him. What do you want?"

"I wonder," Bill said, "if I might see your daughter?"

"Look around," she told him. "You don't see her, do you?"

"No," Bill said. He stood just inside the door.

"Unless you think I've locked her up in the bathroom?" Mrs. Macklin said. "I've got a headache. Think she cares? Up and out before I woke up. Well?"

Mrs. Macklin, Bill decided, was several persons. This one was the morning Mrs. Macklin, sober—but possibly rectifying that—and probably with a hangover.

"All of them're like that," she said. "Always were. Oh, I know. Not as young as they are, just in the way. You'll find out." She took a sip from her glass. "Try the swimming pool," she said. "What do you want to see her about?" She took another swallow, this time larger. "Been up to something?"

"She?" Bill said. "Not that I know of. Mrs. Macklin—" He paused for attention. She said, "Well?" and finished what might have been merely tomato juice—or, of course, a Bloody Mary.

"I understand," Bill said, "that you have some very valuable jewelry with you, Mrs. Macklin. Is it in the purser's safe?"

She put the glass down hard on the table. She put it down so hard that dishes rattled against one another. She said, *"Who told you that?"*

"Is it true?" Bill asked her.

"Is it," she said, "any of your business?"

She had a point there, if she cared to press it.

"Perhaps not," Bill said. "But—you complained that someone had got into your room. If you have valuables in your room—" It was not especially adequate. It seemed somewhat better than to ask, point-blank, if she harbored stolen jewelry of which a murdered man had carried pictures.

"Days ago," she said. "And nobody did anything. You're just getting around to it now?"

Bill Weigand did not argue about the number of days. He said, "Then you haven't valuable jewelry?"

"Young man," she said, "there's nothing the matter with my mind. Hear me? My mind's as good as it ever was."

There seemed to be no answer at all to that.

"About the jewels?" Bill said, and was patient.

"You say you're a policeman," she said. "How do I know you're not trying to steal anything you can lay hands on?"

Bill showed her his badge. She said, "Phooey." She said, "Just because I'm not as young as I was." She made, Bill thought, a great point of it. She might have been ninety from the point she made of it. She was not, he thought, much older than the middle or late sixties. It was surprising that, when she exaggerated, rather than minimized her age, she had gone to the trouble of youthening her face. Or, perhaps it wasn't.

"Have you or haven't you?" Bill said.

"Haven't," she told him, and the dark eyes were narrowed slightly, and there was the suggestion of a smile on the thin lips in the skintight face. "What would I have jewelry for?"

The question was absurd. There was, indeed, a certain absurdity about all of Mrs. Macklin. Or—did she, for some reason, wish to appear absurd? He kept getting questions, Bill thought; questions when he wanted answers. He went in search of Miss Hilda Macklin, who probably would deny that she had, to Aaron Furstenberg, so much as mentioned precious stones. He visited the most likely places—he went past the swimming pool, and to the sun deck—and flicked a hand to his wife and the Norths, and went on. He went to the smoke room, and to the Grand Lounge, and circled the promenade deck. He did not find Hilda Macklin, which was odd, but only a little odd. A ship was, he thought, an easy place on which to hide, if one wanted to hide. It was also an easy place to disappear in, whether one wanted to hide or not. Miss Macklin might be in a women's lavatory, of which there were many. She might be visiting a friend in the friend's stateroom. Probably, Bill decided, he would be as apt to come across Miss Macklin if he sat somewhere in the sun, and waited for her to find him. He joined Dorian and the Norths.

"Hilda Macklin was wearing a white dress," Pam said, sitting upright on her chair, speaking with the air of one who speaks of important things. "A *long* white dress." She waited, her eyes bright with expectancy.

Bill looked at Dorian, at Jerry. Jerry nodded, confirming what Pam had said, clearly sharing her belief that what she said had meaning. And Dorian waited too.

"I came in late," Bill reminded them.

"Last night," Pam said. "It wasn't barebacked, but otherwise—Don't you see? It was almost dark on the deck and a woman in white—" She stopped, as one who did not wish to labor a point.

Bill's first reaction was to reject out of hand, since it was absurd to suppose that, even in semi-darkness, anyone else could be mistaken for Dorian. Or, more precisely, and as Pam was suggesting, Dorian for Hilda Macklin.

"It was quite dark," Pam North said, helping him, recognizing his need for help. "And—they move alike. A little." Bill raised his eyebrows. "Oh," Pam said, "but they do. I remember thinking that yesterday or some time. That Hilda moved almost like Dorian. I told Jerry—didn't I, Jerry?"

"Yes," Jerry said.

"Only that," Pam said. "In the light—I don't say they're at all alike. But in the darkness, or almost— seeing somebody in a white dress, moving in a certain way. Don't you see?"

It was still hard to see. But it was not so hard as it had been at first. Bill's face showed that.

"It makes more sense," Pam said. "Because, who would want to hurt Dorian?"

Dorian said, "Oh come now." She said that she could have enemies as well as anybody, if she put her mind to it. Pam said, "I didn't mean—" and realized herself caught out, and responded to Dorian's smile. "All the same," she said, "it does make more sense."

Bill nodded slowly, and said, "Right." What sense it made was not, to be sure, much clearer. If someone— certainly a very careless someone—had tried to kill Dorian thinking her Hilda Macklin things became, if not clarified, at least not entirely incoherent.

"Look!" Dorian said, and pointed, and there was Morro Castle, looking precisely like its pictures. The

Carib Queen, moving very slowly now, nosed up the channel toward Havana Bay.

The public-address system clicked, and politely asked for attention. It then requested that all who wished to participate in the American Express Company's guided tour of Havana, in private limousines, make their arrangements at the desk in the grand entrance. It paused. It said, "We repeat," and did.

To see a large and unfamiliar city in which the language is strange as the streets are strange, a guided tour is best, although of course faintly repugnant. "I think," Dorian said, "that we ought to swallow our pride," and to that Pam agreed, although pointing out that it would probably entail a great many churches. "To stand in the middle of and look at," she said, amplifying. In spite of this, they sent Jerry forward to arrange for three. Bill would, somehow, overtake them, when he could. They went below to freshen up for Havana. The ship, going ever slower, crept past other piers toward her own—crept past a strange large ship full of freight cars (outbound for Florida) and past low merchant ships, and among bright, darting launches. Now and then, for reasons not apparent to landsmen, the *Carib Queen* hooted, conversationally. At a little after eleven, she tied up. Fifteen minutes later, after what seemed a good deal of fussing, the guard at the head of the gangplank stepped aside and the passengers of the *Carib Queen*—or such of them as did not, thriftily, remain to lunch aboard—surged into Havana. Bill and Dorian were just in time to surge with the others. They had, Bill explained, waited for Dorian to finish a sketch.

Havana was a long pier, with a passageway between stacked crates and bales. Havana was a street, no more grimy, and no less, than all streets which abut on piers. Havana was a line of cars—two of which were limousines, the rest taxis—and three seemingly excited men wearing caps banded with the words "American Express." The men talked very rapidly in what was often English, and apportioned tourists among cars.

They saw Hilda Macklin, then—saw her just as she was whisked into a car in which there were already three other people. Bill tried, without success, to identify the others; thought none of them was Mrs. Macklin, but could not be sure. Almost before Hilda Macklin was seated in the car, its horn blasted and it leaped away, turning violently into a narrow street. "Señors, señoras," a guide urged, and compressed Pam and Jerry North and Dorian into a cab. He reached out for Bill Weigand. Bill shook his head, and went to a waiting police car. The guide shrugged, and said, "Señor?" to Captain J. R. Folsom, who wore an orange-colored shirt, and no jacket and looked very hot indeed. Captain Folsom was propelled into the car with the Norths and Dorian, the door was slammed, the car squawked angrily, shivered and leaped like a cat with its tail stepped on. Moving, the car continued to squawk, as if its tail still hurt.

It darted through narrow streets, frowned down upon by massive buildings. It turned when least expected, its horn protesting angrily. It darted furiously between other cars at intersections; when, as happened infrequently, it was out-squawked, it stood on its fore-wheels and Pam and Dorian, in the back seat, were catapulted into Jerry and Mr. Folsom, in the jump seats. "Uff!" Mr. Folsom said. The cab plunged into the openness of a square, dashed head-on to a curb and stopped, as if it had balked a jump. They unscrambled themselves and climbed out. Folsom said, "Phew!" for all of them, and the small, dark and engaging man at the wheel removed his hand from the horn button, turned to smile brilliantly and said, "Name of Mike."

"What?" Pam said.

"Sí," he said. "Mike. The cathedral. You find me. Name of Mike."

Cars plummeted into the square, on one side of which the cathedral loomed. From dark buildings, from the shelter of colonnades, children popped, to stand with round dark eyes and expressions of enthrallment—and to suggest the purchase of oddments. The square filled with cabs and the tourists of the *Carib Queen* poured out of them, and looked about dazedly, and counted their arms and legs. A small, anxious man under an American Express cap emerged from a limousine, and said, in a voice too big for him, "Ladies and Gentlemen, if you will please try to stay together, yes?"

"I'm sure," Pam said to Dorian and Jerry, "that we're doing our best."

The cathedral—"Columbus Cathedral"—is massive and of stone, with belltowers at either side; it is aged and massive and not, save for its dignity of age, particularly beautiful. They were led into it, and a good deal of the dignity vanished—it is not dim, but lighted. Rather, as Pam North noted—but in a voice low enough for reverence—like a Christmas tree. Electric lights festooned it, outlining doorways, ringing the altar, winking dimly far above. The guide gathered them about; he spoke admiringly of the woodwork, of murals, of sacred paintings. He re-

minded them that the remains of Christopher Columbus had rested in the cathedral for more than a hundred years. He moved them on.

There is much to see in "Columbus Cathedral" and
the American Express Company is diligent. The guide
led his followers from place to place, through the nave
and the transept, into and out of chapels. The followers diminished; men went outside for cigarettes
and neglected to return; women began to complain of
their feet. Cathedrals are very hard on feet.

Dorian—who likes pictures of many kinds—proved
the most diligent of the three, and Jerry, polite, went
with her, on the fringe of the lessening group. Pam
promised to wait for them, where she could sit down,
and admitted that she was not really good at cathedrals. She sat and waited, and the guide's voice grew
fainter in the distance. Folsom passed her, on his way
toward a door, and was taking out a cigarette package
as he passed. The idea of a cigarette was suddenly
very appealing to Pam North and she stood up,
reached into her bag. She, also, began to drift toward a
door.

She passed a chapel, through which, earlier, the
guide and his followers had moved. It was dim; instead
of electric lights, candles burned in it. And, in it, Hilda
Macklin and Jules Barron stood, close together, talking, their voices low. They were drawn a little to one
side, were only just visible in the semi-darkness. It
was, Pam decided, a surreptitious meeting if she ever
came on one. And it was very interesting. She drew
back, into a window embrasure, and gave up thought
of cigarettes. After all, she thought, we're official this
time, or almost. This sudden close association of
purported strangers—there was something intimate

about the way Hilda and Barron stood, the way they talked—was worthy of attention.

She had come in near the end of the conference, if it was a conference. She had hardly withdrawn into the shadow before Hilda and Barron came out of the chapel. They immediately separated. Barron went, apparently, to rejoin the party—a tardy tourist, which he did not much resemble; it was difficult to believe him intensely interested in sacred murals. Hilda, thin and somehow brittle in gray linen suit, went toward an exit, and went quickly. She went, Pam thought, like somebody up to something. She carried a black bag, held tight under an arm.

It was not Pam North's habit to linger when duty calls, or even when it whispers. This had got her into trouble before now. She went after Miss Hilda Macklin, who was surely up to something—and up to it with Jules Barron who, if he had been trying to strike up an acquaintance with Mrs. Macklin's thin daughter, had certainly, and abruptly, succeeded. Pam took out a cigarette and did her best to look like a woman who was simply dying for one.

She was in time to see Hilda Macklin briskly crossing the cobbled square. She was in time to cross it briskly after her. Hilda went down a narrow street, with the air of one who knows where she is going, and Pam went after her, rather wishing—now that she was committed—that *she* knew where she was going and, perhaps, why. She also wished it were cooler; she had not, until then, realized quite how hot it was in Havana. Hilda turned, suddenly, into a passageway.

The buildings of old Havana are massive, and a little dour. They are given to colonnades. Their walls are thick; passageways vanish mysteriously into them.

Following such passages, one may enter a labyrinth—or may come, unexpectedly, on a hidden, shaded patio. The early residents of Havana wisely sought shelter from Havana's almost tropical sun; many of their survivors are somewhat dazed by such glassy buildings as the American Embassy, planned—like the United Nations building it somewhat resembles—to let sun in.

It was cooler in the passageway, once Pam had followed Hilda into it. The walls on either side were close enough to touch with arms outstretched. There were dark openings in the walls, like the openings of caves. In one she passed—following now the click of heels ahead—a brazier burned and several people, including two children, were clustered around it. They did not pay any attention to Pam North.

She came out into a square, walled by buildings. It did not appear that any streets led out of the square, only other passageways. She was in time to see Hilda Macklin going into one, and went after her. It appeared more than ever that Hilda knew where she was going, and this became increasingly important to Pam, who no longer had the faintest idea where she was. Hilda was now not only quarry; she was guide as well. Pam heard Hilda's heels clicking, echoing in the passageway of stone—and heard the staccato clicking of her own heels. So much did the sound echo that Pam had an uneasy feeling that she might, in turn, be being followed. Which was absurd. She hoped.

She came out of the dark tunnel into a narrow street, which at once curved away to the right. The character of the surroundings had somewhat changed; now there were dimly lighted, rather secretive, shops at intervals, where before the buildings seemed to house only cluttered dwellings—and too many people; so many that they could be felt all around, as if the soft breathing of so many were turned palpable. Here, too, in the narrow street, the sun slanted its way. Then it was hot again.

Pam went quickly through the little street, and felt, now, that people were watching her—that North Americans, dressed for touring, wearing clicking heels, were aliens and intruders, and might, as such, be resented. But there was no sign of resentment in the faces or manners of the few Havanese she saw. They looked at her curiously, but without enmity.

Once she had turned the corner of the street, she could see some distance ahead—and could not see Hilda Macklin. The street ended in a building—with colonnades, with ironwork—and had the appearance of a cul-de-sac. Small, somehow secret, shops opened off it—into any of which Hilda might have gone. Pam stopped, to listen, and did not hear Hilda's footsteps, but nevertheless went on, since she had no notion how to go back. She reached the end of the street, and there was a passage through the building. She could not see the end of the passage, but she could not see where else Hilda could easily have gone—unless into one of the shops. Pam went into it. It would, surely, come out somewhere.

She was in it, and found there was a jog in it, and went around the jog. It was not really dark in the passageway—if one looked up, there was the sky; the very blue sky. But it felt dark and now, listening, Pam felt, more than before, and uneasily, that there was the sound of steps behind her. The echo again, she thought, and stopped. And the sound of footsteps behind her did not stop with hers—not for more than a second. Then the sound stopped.

It was a heavier sound—not the sound of a woman's

clicking leather heels. It was that before it stopped—
before someone waited behind her, for her to go on.

She went on. She went on very fast, and found
herself breathing rapidly, nervously. Anything could
happen in this dark passageway—anything that was
not good. She found that she was almost running.
She—

There was an archway on her right and Pam—
pursued, now, not pursuer—turned into it. There was
a door, and she pushed at the door, and it opened into
a large room. In the middle of the room there was an
alligator hanging by its tail.

10

The National Police of Cuba proved as anxious to co-operate as, by telephone, they had promised to be. They were also efficient. Half an hour after the police car—which moved even more rapidly than the Havana taxicabs—had deposited Captain William Weigand at the massive, ancient and ornate building which is police headquarters, electronics as well as policemen were at his call. A signature sped through nothingness toward Worcester and New York; pictures leaped across oceans and radio messages went along, explaining what was wanted. And Bill Weigand, at a desk supplied, read a message from Sergeant Stein—a message which reiterated and amplified. "Confirming our telephone conversations," Stein might have prefaced, but did not. The police of Los Angeles, as requested, had been asked to trace a Mrs. Winifred Ferris, if possible. Bill doubted it would be. The president of the Worcester Box Company, of which J. R. Folsom was treasurer, was one Abner Baldwin, who had not yet proved available.

The waiting game again, as it was so often, Bill

decided, and drummed on the borrowed desk with his finger tips. His opposite number sat at a larger desk.

"It does not go well?" he enquired. Bill said that it did not go particularly well. A telephone rang; there was a conversation in Spanish.

"Miss Macklin," the opposite number said, "has not yet visited Carrillo et Cie."

Where else might she go? The sub-inspector of the Cuban National Police considered. He shrugged. There were many places, if she knew of them. Some as reputable as Carrillo et Cie. Some—again he shrugged. It was improbable that a young North American woman would know of those, unless— There was another shrug. In all large cities, as the captain knew, there were these others. In New York, undoubtedly. Places where one might sell precious stones without too much enquiry—without any enquiry—as to the source from which they came. But, as he understood it, Miss Hilda Macklin would neither know of such dealers, nor have reason to learn of them. The jewels she might wish to sell were her mother's, were they not?

"Presumably," Bill said. "None of it is too clear, inspector."

"A block on a certain street," the sub-inspector said, and named the street. "There we keep a watch but—" He shrugged again. If Captain Weigand wished, men could be sent, with photographs—with this so admirable drawing of Miss Macklin—to the more likely places? In the usual course, such a procedure might come to nothing. But, with murder involved—and to be mentioned? Few like even a remote association with murder.

It would, Bill thought, be worth trying. They waited. Photographs, electronics through with them, came back to the office. They were sent away again, this time to be rephotographed. They waited and while they waited drank coffee, which was black and bitter, and delicious. In his, the sub-inspector used much sugar. The copied sketch, the copied photographs, came back. Bill put them in an envelope. He put Stein's message in an envelope.

He might, Bill said, as well see Havana, since he was in it—since seeing Havana had, when all this was only to be a pleasure cruise, been one of the main points. It would be a privilege to assist Captain Weigand to see their beautiful city; they had special tourist policemen whose English was excellent, whose knowledge of the city complete. It—

Bill was appreciative, realized there would be no other way one half so good. But, he was with a party, including in it, his wife. "The artist," the sub-inspector said, with appreciation. No doubt, the American Express tours had an established itinerary? If Bill could be guided to some likely point where—

He stopped, since a uniformed policeman came in, with urgency in his manner. He spoke, in Spanish and—it appeared—in surprise, to the sub-inspector, who then spoke to Bill Weigand, in English, but also in some surprise. There was a man who wished to see the captain—wished, it appeared, somewhat urgently to see the captain. A Mr. Folsom?

Bill shared the surprise. While they waited for Mr. Folsom, the sub-inspector lifted his dark eyebrows. Bill Weigand shrugged his shoulders.

Respected Captain J. R. Folsom came in, wearing an orange shirt, and looking very hot.

Pamela North, confronted by a dangling alligator, said, *"eeHH!"* on a rising note, and stopped, braced backward. The alligator revolved slowly, as if to regard her—as if in annoyance at this interruption of solitude. It was, however, only the skin of an alligator. "Huh," Pam said, on a declining note. "Pretending to be—"

But then she heard, or thought she heard, the door through which she had come, and had closed behind her, opening again. Pam North went around the alligator, brushing counters on which other alligators, or large sections thereof, were piled, and toward a door beyond. She went through the door briskly, and half a dozen men and women, sitting at tables, looked at her with dark eyes and with astonishment. The four women, and two men, were cutting up alligators.

"Señora," one of the men said, "you come by the back door? It is preferred to come by the front door. Sí?"

"Sí," Pam said. "Sí indeed. Oh—alligator *bags!*"

"Sí," the man said. "The best alligator bags. For almost nothing, señora. But—in front, sí?"

He pointed. Pam North went between tables. She came into a larger room, opening on a street—a room festooned with alligator bags of many sizes, many shapes; of alligator bags suspended, lying on showcases, glassed within showcases. A middle-aged woman, who had been looking through the door into a deserted square, turned abruptly. Large dark eyes grew perceptibly larger.

"Señora?" she said, as if doubting it. "But you came by the back door."

"I know," Pam said. "It—well, I just came to it. That is, it was there."

The woman regarded Pamela North. As others had done before her, she shook her head, as if the movement were reflexive. Then she looked at the door through which Pam had come.

"The others?" she said. "They also—"

"Others," Pam said. "Are there—?"

"American Express," the woman said.

"Oh," Pam said, "Looking at the cathedral."

The woman among the alligator bags continued to regard the door Pam had come through. She looked at it with an expression which mingled expectation and alarm. "It is not like the American Express," she said. "Always they come by the front door. Sí?" She turned back to Pam. "However," she said, "you wish a bag?" She held one up. But Pam did not look at it.

She looked through the open door, into the square. Mr. Jules Barron was coming into the square from a passageway. He was looking around the square.

"I," said Pamela North, "do very much want a bag. Please."

There had never been so many alligator bags. One after another, as the large woman brought them forth, pointed them out, Pam looked at alligator bags. And, between one bag and the next, she looked through the door into the square, where it was clear that Mr. Jules Barron waited for someone. He appeared to wait patiently.

"This one is beautiful, sí?" the large woman said, and produced another. "But perhaps the señora would prefer—"

The trouble was that Pam North does not really much like alligator bags, regarding them as knobby and, in addition, requiring alligator shoes, which she likes even less. "Beautiful," Pam North agreed. "But what I more had in mind was—"

It could not be said that the middle-aged woman

grew impatient. But she did, as minutes passed, appreciably warm to her task. This señora who came through back doors, who looked and looked but without real attention—this señora would leave with an alligator bag, or the reason why would be known. "Nowhere, señora," the woman said, resolutely, "nowhere in Habana will the señora find such a collection as we have here."

Pam did not doubt it. She said she did not doubt it. She looked out the door where Jules Barron, a man with all the time in the world in his unhurried hands, leaned slightly against a column in the shade, and looked as if he belonged there—looked rather, indeed, as if he had grown there.

"It is so hard to decide," Pam said. "They are all so beautiful. This one, now. Or—perhaps this one. Although this one is so—"

She stopped, and stopped pretending not to look through the door into the square. Because, from between two massive buildings, Hilda Macklin came briskly, her black bag—not alligator—clutched under her right arm. She walked across the square, which was cobbled, to Barron and, as she walked, Pam thought Hilda shook her head. Barron moved a few steps to join her, they talked for an instant; side by side, still talking, they walked through a colonnade and disappeared.

"So that's it," Pam said. "Not me at all."

"Señora?" the large woman said. "Which one not you?"

"Oh," Pam said, and slightly shook the alligator she held. "This one, I think. I mean, this one *is* me."

It was not really very cheap. And Pam was sure, or almost sure, she could learn to like it. Or, it would make a nice present for—She could not think of anyone for whom it would make an especially nice present. Pam signed a traveler's check.

And, as she signed it, the square filled with taxicabs, as if they had fallen from the sky. The American Express had come charging to the rescue. The American Express was a little late. Pam looked reproachfully at the too-expensive, knobby bag.

"So," the large woman said, "by the *front* door, as I told the señora."

Respected Captain J. R. Folsom, looking very hot indeed—although it was comparatively cool in the office, behind massive walls—said that anybody could make a mistake. Bill Weigand did not challenge this statement of the obvious. He was asked to look at it Folsom's way and said, "Right, Mr. Folsom. You recognized the signature. You said you didn't."

"Look at it my way," Folsom said, again. "I was rattled. I said I made a mistake."

"You realized," Bill Weigand said, "that once I got ashore, I'd radio the signature to Worcester. That a hundred people there would recognize it. That, once it was identified as Baldwin's, I'd know you'd been lying."

He was told he made it sound bad. Suppose Folsom had got to thinking it over afterward, realized he had made a mistake?

"Like I say," Folsom said, "anybody can. I thought maybe I could keep out of it. Until I thought it over."

"The signature," Bill said, "is Abner Baldwin's. He's president of your company. He'd hired Marsh to—to do what, Mr. Folsom? You may as well—not make another mistake."

"Lil Abner," Folsom said, "is a prize s.o.b. Ask anybody in Worcester."

"Suppose," Bill said, "you just tell me what it's about. Right?"

It took Folsom time, and many suggestions that Weigand look at it his way. It took a history, not too brief, of the Worcester Paper Box Company, which had been the Folsom Paper Box Company—into which Abner Baldwin had "moved," during the depression, after Folsom's father, and the company's founder, had "passed away."

"You have to get the background," Folsom said, and Bill Weigand was patient.

Yet it was not too clear, even when lengthily explained. Baldwin was trying to squeeze; that was what it came to. Trying to get Folsom out, and take over completely. "So, he rigged this thing up. Figures he's got me by the short hair, when all the time he knows it's a phony." In short—but it was not in short— Baldwin had accused Folsom of embezzlement ("which is a g.d. lie and he knows it") and was willing to let it slide if Folsom had consented to be squeezed out. "I told him to go take one," Folsom said. "At you know who."

Bill knew who.

"Put up or shut up," Folsom said, amplifying. "See what I mean?"

Bill saw what he meant.

"He didn't have anything to go on," Folsom said, and Bill Weigand said, "Anything?"

"Nothing he could make stick," Folsom said. "Oh—say somebody came in from the outside. Didn't know the ropes. Until I got him squared away— maybe—" He stopped and looked at Weigand, his gray eyes very sharp—very cold in his hot face. "It could have been rigged so it didn't look so good," he said.

"That's all. So, apparently, he hires this Marsh fellow. To—make it look bad. See what I mean?"

Bill saw what he meant.

"And," Folsom said, "Marsh gets himself killed. You see why I wanted to stay out of it."

"You didn't," Bill said. "You went to Marsh's stateroom."

"We were drinking, like I said," Folsom told him. "Seemed to me he was getting a little nosy. About the company. I said to myself, 'Nobody's that interested in boxes.' I said to myself, 'Lil Abner's up to something and this Marsh is in it.' So, I thought it over and decided I'd have a showdown. Put it up to Marsh. So I went to his room and—there he was. There you and the captain were."

"Right," Bill said. "There we all were."

"And that damned sword," Folsom said. "Sticking up out of the middle of him. Sword I'd had sharpened up."

"Disconcerting," Bill said. "If you didn't use the sword."

"Would I be telling you this, if I had?"

"Perhaps," Bill said. "Since you began to realize I'd find out anyway."

"Anybody can make a mistake," Folsom said. "I didn't kill the guy."

"Or," Bill said, "search my room, and the Norths' room, trying to find the letter and the check—or whatever you thought you might find? And push Mrs. North around while you were about it? Or slug the captain's steward, so you could search Marsh's room? Or—search Mrs. Macklin's room?"

"Nope," Folsom said. "I didn't do a damn' thing. Anyway—" He stopped and looked at Bill. "I stopped by Mrs. Macklin's room to see if I could buy her a drink."

"A bit of detective work?"

"So?"

"I don't know, Mr. Folsom," Bill said. "But I'll find out. The ship sails around ten tomorrow morning. I'd be on it, if I were you."

"Captain," Folsom said, "didn't you know? We're having this parade in Nassau."

Clutching her knobby alligator, Pam went into the square. She encountered Miss Springer, who said, "You're Mrs. North," and said it accusingly. "You are not supposed to wander off," Miss Springer said. "People ought to stay together."

Pam said she was very sorry. She said, "Do you know where my husband is?"

"At the cathedral," Miss Springer said. "Looking for you."

It was a short distance to the cathedral by cab. Jerry, in the square, was talking to a member of the tourist division of the police department, who had an armband which said he was. Jerry said, "Well!" to Pam, and Pam, again, said she was sorry and would explain, and where was Dorian?

"Looking in crypts, probably," Jerry said, but they found Dorian in the nave of the cathedral, which was, now, by no means so gaudily lighted. Together again, the three found Mike and his cab, and Mike did not chide. He said, "Now we catch up." They got in. "Wait," Pam said, "it merely leads to alligator bags. Like—" she showed them. "How much?" Jerry said, and she told him. He said, conventionally, "Ouch!"

"We'll merely have to wait until everybody sees

everything," Pam said. "It takes some people a long time. Mike?"

"Señora?"

"You can just drive us around, can't you? Where the others would go, except not the alligators, but faster?"

"You do not want the bags?" Mike said.

"No," Pam said.

"Then," Mike said, "we see the cemetery, sí? The cemetery is very beautiful."

They saw Colón Cemetery, which, tabled in marble, is not only beautiful but oddly gay. Happy boys were shooting dice on one of the great white slabs. They saw old Havana, passing through it like a whirlwind, with Mike turning back, steering with a hand on the center of the wheel, over the horn button, to advise of beauties passing. They saw new Havana, where much is modern and bright and from the point of view of the climate obviously ill-advised, and now and then not a little funny. They whirled madly through Marianao and past the country club, and in the winding roads on which fine houses wear many colors. Returning, Mike's cab coughed tiredly and stopped on a busy bridge, was pushed to seclusion and repaired with, apparently, a few pieces of old wire kept handy for the purpose. It darted on, speed and voice alike restored, and roared to a stop outside a spreading building. "Rum factory," Mike said, in triumph. "Trocadero." Then the remainder of the American Express tour descended like a flight of locusts. They, with others—and now with Mrs. Macklin who could, Pam noted, be trusted to turn up at the right time—sat on small kegs around large barrels made into tables and drank banana cordial. It was, in its way, remarkable. And Bill came, with a policeman escorting him, and said this was a way to spend their time, while he was slaving over murder, and sipped banana cordial—which was certainly remarkable—with them. He agreed with Pam that it was hard to keep one's mind on murder. They recaptured Mike and whirled to a restaurant of his advising—"where," Pam insisted, "we can get martinis" and scrubbed banana sweetness from her lips with her teeth. It was on the way that Pam said, suddenly remembering, "We've lost Mr. Folsom."

They had not, Bill assured them, over *paella,* and told of Mr. Folsom. In return, he heard of Hilda Macklin and Jules Barron and alligator bags. He left them for a telephone, after Pam had described the street—somewhere near the cathedral, in a labyrinth—where Hilda had disappeared. He returned. "At a guess," Bill said, "it was what they call The Street of Fences."

"Oh," Pam said, and Bill Weigand said, "Right," and they were, once more, out of the brightness of holiday into the darkness of murder. "Checkers must feel like this," Pam said, "or chessmen, of course," and after she had explained they agreed that either might well.

In mid-afternoon, heavy with *paella,* they went back to the *Carib Queen,* where the others rested and Bill Weigand did not.

Gloomily, since he had still no hunch, and could see none in immediate prospect, Bill Weigand went again to the telephone. He had never, he thought, while waiting the connection, tried to discover who had killed and why under conditions less satisfactory. The past remained obscure; the present was in a state of flux; unaccustomed *paella* lay heavy on the stomach and seemed to weight the brain.

"Stein, Homicide West," a distant voice—and a weary voice—said and then, "Oh, hello, captain, where do I begin?"

"Anywhere," Bill said.

Then—the signature on the letter, and on the check, was that of one Abner Baldwin, president of the Worcester Paper Box Company. Bill said, "Right," and Stein, somewhat disappointed, said that it sounded as if his news were old. Bill told him. And what had Mr. Baldwin to say?

Baldwin had been at first reluctant, had ended somewhat vociferous. Or so, as reported by a Worcester detective, it appeared. "We're a long way from everything," Bill said, wearily. "Go ahead."

Baldwin had said it was something he didn't want the police in. He was told why the police were in. He agreed that that changed matters. He agreed that he had employed J. Orville Marsh to investigate Folsom. It was then he had begun to grow vociferous; had said he was pretty sure the damned crook was robbing him. He had then turned cautious. He had said that maybe he shouldn't say what he couldn't prove—couldn't prove yet. He had diverged to remark, bitterly, that Marsh had been a sap to get himself killed with the job half done. That now he would have to get somebody else to start over.

"Too bad he's been inconvenienced," Bill said, and Stein said it sure was.

Baldwin failed, or said he failed, to see what Marsh expected to gain by following Folsom on a cruise—particularly as he supposed that eventually, from somewhere, there would be an expense bill to cover the cruise. Pressed—but not hard enough; not nearly hard enough; that much was evident—Baldwin said that Folsom seemed to have been juggling his accounts, in cahoots with a supplier of cardboard. At least, it appeared that there ought to be a lot more cardboard around than there really was. But he didn't have enough on Folsom to take it to the police. That had been where Marsh came in.

That, so far, was all from Baldwin—from Worcester and the Worcester Paper Box Company.

"Too bad you couldn't have gone up yourself," Bill said, and was agreed with. "Take it up with Arty when you get back," Stein suggested. "Oh," Bill said, "sure. I can see myself. The other things?"

The photograph found among Marsh's effects was of Mrs. Winifred Ferris of Cambridge, Massachusetts. Her son and her daughter agreed to that. It had been taken some time previous to her disappearance; had been given to Marsh to direct him in his search. The jewelry of the photographs also was hers. Mrs. Ferris's son had had the photographs made. "Why? Or didn't they think to ask?"

The detective assigned had thought to ask. He had been told "as a safeguard," and had waited. Ferris had hesitated; finally, with apparent reluctance, had said his mother was "sometimes" a little irresponsible. The pieces were very valuable; it might, he thought, some time be necessary to identify them.

"Meaning?"

Stein supposed that, in an "irresponsible" moment, Mrs. Ferris might lose her jewels. Or give them away. Her son and daughter had wanted to be in a position, if the pieces subsequently were found, to prove their identity. "Hmmmm," Bill said. "It's all he could get," Stein said. "He seems to know his way around. The cop, I mean." Bill knew what he meant. The son and daughter presumed that Mrs. Ferris had taken the pieces with her. She had kept them in a safe deposit box, to which she alone had access.

"They haven't tried to get a court order?"

They had, the investigating detective thought, been thinking of it, but then the letter came from their mother in California. With that proof of her existence, and good health, nobody would give them an order.

Bill said, "Mmmm." Then he said, "The Ferrises. How do they seem to be fixed? Tycoon types?"

Not that, Stein had gathered; not anywhere near that. Ferris—Walter Ferris—was an office manager; held a good-enough job, but not the sort on which one grew rich. All the same, Stein gathered—although the point had not sharply arisen—that the Ferrises were well-enough heeled.

"Otherwise," Stein said, "what would they—the family, that is—be doing with this here now fortune in jools?"

"You'll be coming around the mountain when you come, sergeant," Bill said. "We don't really know there is one. Any other thoughts?"

"Only," Stein said, "that if she's in California, she's not your Mrs. Macklin. I suppose that's what you're after?"

"I'm damned," Bill said, "if I know what I am after. The sketch?"

The Ferrises were of two minds about a sketch Dorian had made—in which Dorian had tried to visualize a face as it had been before plastic surgery had relentlessly tightened skin over bone. Walter Ferris had thought it might be his mother's. His sister—and his wife—had thought not.

"It isn't too much like the photograph," Stein said.

"Dorian tried to keep the photograph out of her mind," Bill said. "There'd have been no use in it otherwise. She may have tried too hard, I suppose. Go ahead."

"That's about all, so far," Stein said. "He asked again about the possibility of another child—Mrs. Ferris's, I mean. Nope. Just the two. Asked around a little among neighbors, that sort of thing. Got a few of them to agree that Mrs. Ferris might be considered a little eccentric. Nice way of putting it. But—not forthcoming. Don't like people's affairs pried into. And—"

He stopped. Bill could hear him, faintly, face obviously turned from the receiver, say, "All right. Let's have it." Bill waited. "Something from L.A.," Stein said. "Hold on." Bill held on.

"Well," Stein said, on the telephone again, "looks like our Mrs. Ferris is in L.A., all right. Or was, anyhow, as late as Saturday."

Bill Weigand, his tone resigned, told Sergeant Stein to go ahead. Then—

Approximately ten days before, a Mrs. Winifred Ferris, of Cambridge, Massachusetts, had checked into the Midtown Plaza in Los Angeles. The previous Saturday—"day before yesterday, that is"—she had checked out again. The hotel was large. The Los Angeles police had not, as yet, found anybody who remembered Mrs. Ferris in any detail. A chambermaid had seen her once or twice, and recalled her as middle-aged. The clerk to whom she had paid her bill, and surrendered her key, did not remember her at all. Why should he? People came and went.

"We can wire the photo out," Stein said. "Probably won't come to anything. Trouble is, people don't look at people."

That, Bill agreed, was a trouble. But a more immediate trouble was: If Mrs. Ferris was checking out of a Los Angeles hotel on Saturday, she could not very well be Mrs. Macklin, who had sailed aboard the *Carib Queen* from New York on Friday.

"Funny business," Stein said, but he said it doubtfully.

There was always, Bill agreed, a chance of funny business. Funny business they had always with them. But—why? What would make it worth the trouble?

Sergeant Stein had no answer. Nor had he, for the moment, further information. He left Bill Weigand to his thoughts, which were discouraging. Things seemed constantly to slip through his fingers. It appeared, now, that Mrs. Ferris had slipped, leaving him with Respected Captain Folsom. Folsom was, certainly, a possibility. But Folsom did not "feel" right. The more Bill thought of it, looking at, without seeing, the silent telephone, the more unpleasantly possible seemed the chance that he was on the wrong track altogether. (Not, he thought, with waxing irritation, that he was on any clear track whatever, or had been.) Neither Mrs. Ferris nor Mr. Folsom might have anything to do with the matter. Marsh might have been killed for reasons quite unknown, by persons undreamed of. Miss Springer, the social hostess, for example. Perhaps Mr. Marsh had spurned Miss Springer. Bill Weigand was stern with himself. Undoubtedly, overindulgence in *paella* was to blame.

He clung to a bracelet, two necklaces and a ring, presumably of great value. He clung to the probability that Hilda Macklin, in her journey through narrow streets of old Havana, trailed by Pamela North, had sought to dispose of jewelry—perhaps had disposed of jewelry. He did not know that it was the jewelry of which Marsh had carried photographs. He had not seen it; Hilda had described it to Aaron Furstenberg only in general terms. The articles might be different altogether. He thought it probable, if not certain, that Jules Barron had recognized the photographs. It was probable, not certain, that Hilda and Jules Barron were in something together. (They might, of course, merely have struck up a shipboard acquaintance. Hilda might have asked his advice, as she had asked Furstenberg's. There was nothing to prove that Barron had followed Pam while she was following Hilda, finally among alligators. There was nothing to prove anything.)

Bill Weigand went in search of stimulation. He went to his stateroom, and found Dorian in siesta, and very pretty in it. There is nothing, on a cruise, like a good afternoon nap. . . .

They met by pre-arrangement, in the smoke room, at a little after seven. They found the big room cool, and almost deserted. They found Captain Peter Cunningham, out of uniform, in a white linen suit, having a gin and tonic. "Ship's tied up," Captain Cunningham said, indicating the drink. "Find Havana a bit of a bore?"

They did not, Pam told him, for the others—they most certainly did not. They had merely come aboard to nap. Thereafter they would go into the city and be gay. "Perhaps," Pam said, "even a night club. Although we almost never do at home."

They must not miss one of the night clubs, Captain Cunningham agreed. He named several. He was, and this seemed a little to surprise him, going to one himself—club called The Castle. With Mr. and Mrs. Furstenberg—a new club, in the Sans Souci area, said to be very good. Then Captain Cunningham looked at Bill Weigand, and raised his eyebrows.

"A good many things," Bill said, and told him some of them.

"Beats me how you sort 'em out," Cunningham said. "Wouldn't know which way to turn, in your place."

The Furstenbergs came into the smoke room and looked around it, and Cunningham said, "Probably meet up later," and went to join them.

"When you're on to something," Pam said to Bill Weigand, "you look different. You don't look different."

There had been, Bill said, nothing to make him. He told them what Stein had reported.

"It looks to me," Jerry said, "as if you're left with Mr. Folsom."

"It looks to me at the moment," Bill said, "as if I'm left with everybody." He turned to Pam. "By this time," he said reproachfully, "you've usually stirred things up."

"I," Pam said, "have been thrown about. I have been chased in dark alleys. I—" She stopped suddenly. "I suppose," she said, "that Mr. Furstenberg really is?"

They waited a moment. Then, cautiously, Jerry said, "Is what, Pam?"

"Why," she said, "Mr. Furstenberg, of course. All we know is what he says. Or?"

"No," Bill said, "I haven't checked. There is a Furstenberg, certainly. Whether this *is* Furstenberg—why?"

"Impostor," Pam said. "Marsh really knew him—that is, knew the real Mr. Furstenberg. So this one had to kill him." She looked at the others. "All I offer is a straw," Pam said. "All is not gold that glisteneth. Or diamonds either, of course. And—" She stopped;

looked at Bill Weigand. "You've thought of something," she said, with accusation. "Instead of listening—"

She continued to look at him.

"The jewelry isn't really?" she said. "But how would that—"

"No," Bill Weigand said. "I wasn't thinking of that. But—I thought the diamond sparkle may have got in our eyes."

They waited. Bill did not continue.

"It is not," Dorian said, at length, "like you to be cryptic."

"The sea air," Bill said.

"More likely," Dorian said, "all that *paella* you had for lunch."

Bill grinned at that. He stood up. He said he would be gone only a minute, and they looked up at him.

"Radiogram I want to send," Bill told them, and the smile remained widely on his face. He went.

"Exactly," Pam North said, "like the Cheshire cat."

11

They went, in time, from the ship and through the pier warehouse and into the soft night. "I wait," Mike said, standing by his taxicab, patting it with affection. "As you say, I wait." They had not said anything about Mike's waiting, but his brown eyes glowed with what was, presumably, devotion.

"Si," Jerry said.

"The night is beautiful," Mike told them, with rather the air of one who has invented darkness. "She is not so hot."

She was not; she was a warm, almost a tender night, but she was not hot. They got into Mike's taxicab and plunged through the warm night of Havana, amid prodigious squawks. They dashed up to, seemed about to carom off, a restaurant, and found it gay and bright and partially filled. It was only a little after eight, and they were early, and had expected to be, and did not mind. They were welcomed; not even their expressed preference for martinis to daiquiris marred the welcome. The waiter only slightly frowned, and instantly recovered himself.

189

They had steaks and fried green bananas and did not hurry; they had dessert and black Spanish coffee, and did not hurry. They asked Bill to whom, about what, he had sent a radiogram (with the air of one to whom something has just occurred) and were asked to bide their time, and bided it. It was after ten—and the restaurant was by then comfortably filled—when they went again into the night. "I have waited," Mike told them, in triumph. He waited further, briefly, while Bill Weigand made a telephone call.

"The Castle Club," Jerry said, and Mike glowed and said, "She is beautiful, the Castle Club." He bowed them into the cab. They plunged away. Mike turned back, his left hand on the horn button, his smile entrancing. "She is also far," he said, and, apparently without looking, swerved around a bus. The bus snorted at him; the cab squawked in derision. At the bridge across the Almendares River, where earlier the cab had sickened, the motor coughed momentarily. Mike stamped a foot sternly on the floor boards. The car, chastened, ceased to cough. They darted on a broad avenue through what was, they presumed, Marianao; they swirled past the country club; they darted among the curving streets of the Sans Souci district. Beyond question, she was far.

The Castle Club was at first a glow around a bend. Averting eyes from road, turning to face his passengers, Mike spoke in triumph. "The Castle Club!" he told them, with the simple pride of a man who owns it. He pressed his hand on the horn button for emphasis, and the car squawked obediently. It found, or seemed to find, its own way around the bend. It avoided, as if by instinct, a car approaching from the opposite direction. It went faster.

The glow came from vari-colored floodlights, affixed

to palm trees. Soft reds, soft yellows—and a few gay pinks—brightened the frond plumes. It was at once expected, obvious, and beautiful. Above the trees, above the lights, the crystal, seemingly breakable, three-quarters' moon floated in a dark sky. "My!" Pam North said, paying tribute to the spectacle. "She is beautiful," Mike said. "Si?"

The cab swirled in among the palm trees, and the Castle Club seemed to leap, sparkling, from the trees. The builders of the Castle Club, it was instantly apparent, had let themselves go.

The building was low and spreading, and was illuminated by moderate floodlights. It was intensely modern and slightly serpentine in outline. At the entrance, a curved roof of glass defied gravity and the tensile strength of materials. On either side of the entrance, glass walls curved away, into semi-darkness, among the vari-colored palm trees. And, behind the low building—which did a little seem to float—Morro Castle, bathed in pale green light, challenged the dark sky.

"It," Dorian Weigand said, "is not reticent, is it?"

"Si," Mike said. "She is beautiful."

"What on earth," Jerry North said, "is Morro Castle doing here?"

"My!" Pam said, having previously committed herself.

"Señors! Señoras!" a man in uniform exclaimed gladly, and flung the cab door open.

"ScrEEch!" the cab door said, in anguish.

"One day," Mike said, "you will break it off. I will wait."

"Do that," Bill said.

They went into the club, and were passed from hand to hand—and, in addition to the trained cordiality of maitre d's and waiter captains, there was a rather special, somewhat enfolding, warmth in their greeting.

"Of course," Jerry said for his wife's ear, "it is off season."

"Always deflating," Pam said, in a happy voice, feeling suddenly very gay. "As for me, I feel eighteen."

"The patio," the maitre d' told them, and led them through a spreading foyer. To the right of the foyer was a room in which a croupier chanted his litany, in which dice skidded along a table, bounced from a cushioned baffle and were announced. "Messieurs et mesdames," the croupier said. "Messieurs et—"

To the left, behind glass doors, there was a spreading room with tables, with a dance floor in the center— and with nobody in it.

"Tonight the patio," the maitre d' repeated, and they went down broad stairs and into the night—the gayest, brightest of nights. Slender dark girls, wearing nothing in particular with incredible grace, swayed and bucked, in the company of dark young men who wore straw hats, white trousers and what appeared to be abbreviated white nightshirts. Heads tossed and feet stamped, and the girls, from whom feather trains depended, whisked their feathered tails. Feverishly, from beyond the dancers, under a curved glass canopy, an orchestra in bright shirts and slashed trousers played what must surely be the fastest mamba in the world.

Around the dancers there were tables, not all of them occupied. The maitre d' skirted the dancers, stopped proudly at a table for four on the edge of the dance floor and spread his hands in triumph. "Ringside!" he announced and pulled out chairs. They arranged themselves. "By the way," Bill Weigand said, "I'm expecting a message."

The maitre d' eyebrows rose. "A message, señor?" he said, "But of course, a message." He looked with doubt at Pamela, at Dorian; then, with even greater doubt, at Bill Weigand. "A—ah—a message, señor? From another—ah—that is to say—"

"No," Bill said. "Not from a lady. From the police." He looked at the maitre's face. "There will," Bill told him, gravely, "be no disturbance." Then Bill gave his name.

The maitre's face brightened. He nodded and nodded again. A clever one, the maitre's face said. I understand, señor. The señor is discreet. The señor may rely on the discretion of the Castle Club. (The maitre had a talkative face.)

The floor show subsided into the wings, and the band played on. The crystal moon floated high in the dark sky, and was accompanied by stars. And, to one side of the patio, Morro Castle continued to loom darkly. But now it was understandable, being a replica—a sturdy replica, mounting fifty feet into the night air, but by no means so massive as Havana's harbor-guarding emblem. It was not even, in its massiveness—its pale green massiveness—particularly inappropriate to the modernity from which it jutted. About the whole idea there was a certain engaging impertinence.

While the show was on, the table area had been in semi-darkness. Now, with spotlights diminished on the dance floor, it was easier for them to look around. The patio, if occupied to the dusky tables at the perimeter, would hold, perhaps, a hundred and fifty. It was about half filled, and largely—which was pleasant—by undoubted Habaneros. But fellow tourists from the *Carib Queen* were numerous. Most were no more than dimly familiar faces. But the Buckleys were there, at a table for two, looking somewhat round-eyed. (The girls who had danced had really worn very little—far less than is commonly worn in Kansas.) And, part way around the dance floor, Captain Peter Cunningham, RNR, sat at a table with Mr. and Mrs. Aaron Furstenberg. There was a bottle of scotch in the center of the table.

The orchestra put out cigarettes. The orchestra embarked on a rumba—a very fast rumba.

"Come on," Pam said to Jerry, who looked at her in horror. "One two three pause," Pam said, "or anything that comes to mind." She looked at him. "No," she said, "it's not too fast. Come." He went. It was much too fast; it was impossible to remember one two three pause. It, nevertheless, got into the feet, which did something—although certainly not what was prescribed—on their own. Jerry was told he was doing beautifully, and almost believed it.

After a pause, and a second dance, they went back, and were a little breathless. Dorian and Bill were not at the table. In the center of the table, there was a bottle of Vat 69. On the table was a bowl of ice, and bottles of club soda, and four glasses. "Scotch?" Pam said, in doubt, and then looked around at other tables. Most of the tables, and all those occupied by passengers of the *Carib Queen*, were similarly supplied. Dorian and Bill returned, from the vicinity of the dance floor. Pam North pointed at the bottle.

"The custom," Bill said. "We buy a bottle of whisky. We stay as long as we like."

"We will never," Dorian said, "drink half of it."

"That," Bill said, "is probably part of the idea. Takes the place of a cover charge. It—"

He stopped. They looked in the direction he was looking. The maitre d' was bringing further guests—

bringing Respected Captain J. R. Folsom and Mrs. Macklin. The captain had entered into the spirit of things. He wore one of the short white nightshirts. They were, perhaps, more appropriate to slenderer men. Mrs. Macklin, who seemed—at any rate from a distance—to be entirely sober, wore a white dress and her improbably red hair was meekly in order. There was, however, nothing meek about her manner, as she preceded Captain Folsom to a table, a little way back from the dance floor.

"H-mmm," Pam North said. "I wonder—"

They looked at her, and waited.

"That's just it," Pam said. "I don't know what to wonder. It's very baffling."

The orchestra played again. The Norths and Weigands changed partners; they danced again. One of the dancers, with a blond girl from the ship—with the girl who spent so much time in the swimming pool, but seemingly attached to a small boy—was Jules Barron. He was very dark, very Spanish, and a most expert dancer. And Miss Springer, in a white dress which was really much too fluffy, danced with Adjutant Hammond Jones, who was in uniform, and perspiring freely and having not a little trouble with his feet.

The orchestra quit playing, and this time with finality. The orchestra left its glass-roofed enclosure, and went elsewhere. Dancers drifted back to tables. The Norths and the Weigands filled glasses and sipped from them, and watched Miss Hilda Macklin come down the wide stairs into the patio, the maitre d' accompanying her, and helping her look around. They hesitated; then Hilda, who wore the white dress she had worn the night Dorian was pushed, made a motion with her head, had it approved by the maitre d', and went among tables to that at which her mother and Folsom were seated. Folsom stood up while Hilda sat down. She leaned toward Mrs. Macklin, and began to say something.

"Everybody's here," Pam said, and then a waiter came and held out a folded paper to Bill Weigand and said, "Señor Weigand?" making the name sound strangely Spanish. Bill took the paper and unfolded it, and read and nodded his head. "You," Pam said, "are acting like Sherlock. Always picking up things and looking superior."

"Not at all," Bill said, and handed her the paper. She read it aloud. She read: " 'Both affirmative. Stein.' "

"I have never," Dorian Weigand said, "known you to be so aggravating. I'll never take you cruising again."

"I asked the sergeant two questions," Bill said. "Entirely obvious questions, under the circumstances. The answer is affirmative." He regarded them. "There is nothing up my sleeve," he said.

Another band filed into the orchestra's hooded space. It was North American. After they had listened a moment, Jerry said, to Pamela, "Come," and led her away from the dance floor. She was docile, and they walked out among tables. There was no barrier, nothing to delimit the patio from what seemed to be a park surrounding the Castle Club. They walked among palm trees, and found a bench and sat on it. "Why, *Jerry!*" Pam said, after a time, and was told by Jerry that he, also, felt like eighteen again. They looked up at the imitation Morro Castle which loomed above them. After a further time, they left the bench and floated—it was a night for floating—to the tower. An area around the base of the tower was paved with flagstones. There was a door let into the tower and, by the door, a sign, in English and in Spanish. In English, it read: "An excellent view may be obtained from the observation platform."

"It does not," Jerry said, "say of what."

He looked in. Electric lights followed a spiraling staircase. He looked at Pam.

"No," Pam said, and they went elsewhere. They went, again after a time—there was no hurry about anything; time stood still and, apparently, investigation stood with it—back to the table and found Dorian and Bill gone. Gone, too, from their table, were Folsom and Mrs. Macklin, and Mrs. Macklin's thin, undecorated daughter. The music had quieted, and Pam and Jerry danced. When the dance ended, Dorian and Bill Weigand had still not reappeared, and now the Furstenbergs and Captain Cunningham also had vanished. They were not, had not been, on the dance floor. But Jules Barron stood at the edge of the dance floor, alone, looking around him.

"The blonde that got away," Pam said, of that, and then, "Where is everybody?" and, answering herself without hesitation, "In that gambling place," and stood up. Jerry was just perceptibly slow in rising. "Oh," Pam said, "just to look. And it's perfectly legal in Cuba."

She led the way. From outside the gaming room, it appeared that "everybody" including Bill and Dorian Weigand had decided to look. The Weigands were standing near, but not at, a roulette table, and Captain Cunningham was with them. And not far away, Hilda Macklin stood, apparently, as so often, by herself. She was looking fixedly at her mother, and at J. R. Folsom, neither had come merely to watch. Mrs. Macklin put a neat stack of chips on even and another on red.

"Messieurs et mesdames, faites vos jeux," the croupier said, and spun the wheel, and the ball swirled in it. *"Rien ne va plus,"* the croupier said, in the ritual, and after a moment the ball stopped. "Fifteen, odd and black," the croupier said, abandoning the ritualistic for the comprehensible. He then took Mrs. Macklin's chips.

Hilda Macklin looked around the room. Her eyes hesitated a moment, or seemed to hesitate, on Bill Weigand. She moved, then, toward her mother, but checked that movement. Mrs. Macklin opened her purse and looked into it and went to the bank's counter and took out bills and came back with chips. Hilda did go to her then, and touched her shoulder and said something in a low voice. Mrs. Macklin's shoulder moved resentfully, and Hilda took her hand from it and drew back and, again, looked around. There was, Pam North thought, anxiety in the girl's thin face.

Mrs. Macklin leaned over the table and peered at it. Then she quartered on 14, 15, 17 and 18 and put chips again on even, and, just as the wheel started, with a flurried movement, on the second column. *"Rien ne va plus,"* the croupier said, and the wheel stopped. "Four, even, black, first eighteen," the croupier said, and Mrs. Macklin won on even and lost elsewhere. She piled chips with nervous fingers, and again Hilda touched her shoulder. Mrs. Macklin turned, then, with a quickness which shook loose—shook further loose—her improbably red hair. "Leave me alone," Mrs. Macklin said. "You hear? Leave me alone." Hilda drew back, and Mrs. Macklin leaned over the table, holding chips in long, anxious fingers.

The Norths had joined Dorian and Bill and the captain, and found that they, also, were watching Mrs.

Macklin—watching as, now, she wagered on odd and black, and put five chips on each. "I suppose," Pam said, "that they are using real money?"

"The lady," Captain Cunningham said, "is using ten dollar chips."

"But didn't—" Pam said.

"Quite," Captain Cunningham said, looking down at her.

"—her daughter tell Mr. Furstenburg?"

"Right," Bill Weigand said. "She did indeed, Pam. According to Mr. Furstenberg."

"Then," Pam said, and both men shrugged.

"—thirteen, odd and black," the croupier said, and his rake worked quickly over the board, and pushed chips to join Mrs. Macklin's. Her nervous fingers stacked the chips, started to pull them toward her. Then, hurriedly—so that one stack was broken and a chip rolled and had to be retrieved—she pushed them back to odd and black. And from the other end of the table, beyond the wheel, a young, excited voice said, "Wow!" They looked at Mrs. Carl Buckley from Kansas, whose eyes were wide open and her mouth too. She was looking at Aaron Furstenberg, whose expression was unchanged, who looked neither triumphant nor surprised, and still by no means smug, as the croupier pushed three stacks of ten chips each toward him and added five. Mr. Furstenberg had wagered ten dollars on thirteen.

"It seems," Pam said, "like a very nice game."

"No," Jerry said.

They watched, over intervening heads and between them, while Mr. Furstenberg quartered on 13, 14, 16 and 17, and on three other sets; they listened while the croupier chanted, while the little ball rattled gayly in the spinning wheel. "Seventeen, odd and black," the croupier said and now, at two to one, Mrs. Macklin had pleasant stacks of chips in front of her, and Mr. Furstenberg, at eight to one on his quartering, less his losses, also garnered. Mrs. Macklin clawed the chips toward her, and her tight-drawn face was flushed. Mr. Furstenberg's manner was unchanged. Hilda Macklin turned abruptly and went out of the gaming room.

Outside, under the crystal moon, among the many-colored palm trees, the Cuban orchestra was playing again. Music came through the open door. The spinning ball seemed to dance to mamba rhythm.

But the room of roulette, of blackjack, of dice tables, slowly filled. The tinkle of chip on chip, the faint rattle of the little ball, the soft thud of dice against the backing cushion—and the encouraging yelps of the dice players—supplied the more entrancing music. A few of those playing were Cubans, for the most part Cuban men, some in the crisp white pleated nightshirts which, now, Captain Cunningham identified as *guayaberas*. But the Cubans were out-numbered by people from the *Carib Queen*. Around the roulette table, there were now no vacant places—and now a player, unlucky enough to leave for a replenishment of chips, returned bright-eyed and hopeful to find no space to get his money down; was sometimes, indeed, forced to cash in again and go out into the gay night and find what recompense he could in music and the soft gurgle of scotch from bottle.

The Weigands and the Norths had circulated slowly from the immediate vicinity of the roulette table, being partly pushed and partly drawn by a growing realization that something rather special was going on at one of the crap tables. It was not that it was noisy there; it was, on the other hand, rather quieter than at the other tables where dice bounced. But there was a kind of tenseness in the hush around the table, and there was a slow, somehow impressed, drifting toward it. Close enough, they discovered that Respected Captain J. R. Folsom had the dice—and that, apparently, he had had them for some time. They were not bothering with chips at the crap table. Bank notes sufficed. In front of Mr. Folsom there were many bills, loosely piled. And Mr. Folsom's normally ruddy face was oddly white.

Folsom shoved out a sheaf of bills, apparently without counting them. He waited—he waited for some time. The bet was covered. He shook the dice in his hand, sent them tumbling down the table, bouncing from the backboard. They rolled, danced on their corners. They came up three and four, and Folsom, paler than before, drew bills toward him, then pushed them back. "Let it ride," he said. It took longer this time. "Never saw anything like it," a man next to Jerry North said. "Not since Army payday. Ten he makes it?"

Jerry North shook his head. "I just," he said, "bought a very expensive alligator." The man looked at him, and drew away slightly. Mr. Folsom clicked the dice in his hand. This time he blew on them before he sent them dancing down the table. The dice bounced back. A four came up and the other dice pirouetted on its corners. It turned up deuce. The man who had never seen anything like it edged back to Jerry North, alligator or no alligator. "Ten he doesn't," the man offered. Jerry grinned again, shook his head again. "Ten he does," Pamela North said, around Jerry, and the man said, "Done, lady."

Folsom blew on the dice and rolled again, and threw a four and a five. He threw again, and threw eight. He curled his fingers inside his right hand, as if to dry the palm, and blew again on the dice and took a deep breath and waited an instant and rolled them. They bounced back. He threw two treys and said, "Phew," and pulled the money toward him. It appeared to be a great deal of money. He straightened bills between his hands, and looked at the dice. He picked them up and looked at them, and handed them—gently, as if they were precious and very fragile—to the man on his left. "They are all yours, brother," Respected Captain J. R. Folsom said, with a touch of reverence in his voice, and backed away from the table with his hands full of money. He did not wait to see the man on his left throw double six—the fatal "boxcars"—and groan over his evil fate. Mr. Folsom did not, as he went through the crowded room, pushing money into pockets, his face slowly regaining its normal hue, seem to see anybody.

"Here you are, lady," the man who had never seen anything like it said, and held a ten dollar bill out to Pam North. "Oh," Pam said, "did I win?" He merely looked at her. "Well," Pam said, "it's very nice of you," and took the bill. "Alligators!" the man said, and went away. A good many left the dice table, now that Folsom's run was over, and Pam and Jerry and Dorian—Bill had somehow disappeared in the crowd, as had Captain Cunningham—drifted with the others. They found Bill near the door. Dorian put an arm through his, said, "It's better outdoors." But Bill said, softly, "Wait," and pulled her to the side, and turned his back on the door. Pam and Jerry stepped, with them, a few feet farther into the room.

Jules Barron came into the room. He walked across it to the roulette table. Then he moved behind Mrs. Macklin and stood watching the play. He stood there while Mrs. Macklin, who had very few chips in front of her, risked them on even. The croupier said, "Five, red, odd," and the rake gathered in Olivia Macklin's chips.

Her hair was in great disorder, now. Her tight-skinned face was tighter drawn and, as she turned, her black eyes seemed strangely sightless. She got up from the table and, opening her handbag as she went, walked toward the bank counter. She took out bills at the counter.

And, as she left her place, Jules Barron moved quickly into it. A man who had been waiting longer said something they could not hear, and Barron shrugged, as if he did not understand.

Hilda Macklin came to the door of the gaming room and looked into it—looked at the roulette table. Without any change in the expression of her thin face, her almost colorless face, she turned and went back into the foyer.

"Wait," Bill said. "Watch them."

They watched. Jules Barron put two chips on black and the wheel spun. But, instead of staring at the spinning wheel, as most did—as if they could stare it into conformity—Barron looked across the room toward Mrs. Macklin at the counter. "—and black," the croupier said, and pushed two chips to join Barron's two. Barron did not pick them up.

Mrs. Macklin turned from the counter and walked back to the table. Her black eyes were, now, very sharp. Yet she walked to the place where she had played and did not, until she had reached it, stood behind Barron, seem to realize that her place was gone. When she did, she touched Barron on the shoulder, and said something.

He did not turn. His shoulders moved only slightly,

in a shrug. She tapped his shoulder, and then he moved his head in a quick, impatient gesture, and said something which they could not hear.

"Rien ne va plus," the croupier said, and the little ball bounced in the spinning wheel, and now Barron, like the others, seemed to have eyes for nothing else.

"—and black," the croupier said, and his rake moved over the table, and four more chips joined Barron's four. This time he picked two of them up.

Mrs. Macklin took both of his shoulders and pulled at them. "Young man!" she said, and her voice was high, now; now her voice carried above the other voices in the room. "Get up and—"

The croupier made the faintest motion of his head. He said, *"Messieurs et mesdames, faites vos jeux,"* and seemed unperturbed as bets were placed.

"My place," Mrs. Macklin said, and her voice was very high and shrill. "Show you you—"

"—and black," the croupier said, as the wheel stopped.

Barron reached out and took two more chips from the board. He stacked those that remained. He paid no attention to Mrs. Macklin, although still she pulled at his shoulders.

A man in a white dinner jacket—a man with a young-old face and dark eyes which said nothing—came behind Mrs. Macklin. He touched her shoulder, very gently, with great politeness. He smiled, and the smile was pleasant. He said something in a low voice, and she turned and raised a sudden thin hand and plunged it into her disordered, improbable hair. The man's lips moved, and the smile remained. But his hand tightened a little on her shoulder. Across the room, they could see it tighten.

And they could see her body tense; could see the hand come down from her hair and, like the other, clench into a fist. The man's smile did not change; his eyes did not change. He seemed unconscious of the tenseness of the tight-faced woman, although he looked down at her. His lips moved again, very slightly.

Then, after an instant in which the tenseness of her body seemed to increase, Mrs. Macklin shrugged her shoulders, very slightly. He moved aside and she walked back to the bank's counter and stacked chips on it, and for the chips received bills—not many bills. The man in the white dinner jacket had walked behind her to the counter. Now, with the same smile, he stepped aside and bowed. Mrs. Olivia Macklin walked, very straight, toward the door. She did not seem to see the Norths and the Weigands near it. Like Folsom before her, she did not seem to see anybody. She went out of the gaming room.

"All very smoothly done," Jerry North said. "All very much under control."

"Oh," Bill said. "Right. The government keeps an eye on things. Well—" But then he looked back at the roulette table. The wheel had stopped again.

"—and red," the croupier said, and his rake came out and Barron's were among the chips garnered by the house. Barron watched them go and seemed without interest. He looked at the door through which Mrs. Macklin had gone. He stepped back, then, and nodded and smiled at the man who had waited longer. The man moved in. Barron walked to a dice table and stood looking at the play, but he made no offer to join it.

"The daughter had him come?" Pam said.

Bill hesitated for a moment. Then he said, "Yes. I think so. You might put it that way."

12

They walked through the foyer and down the shallow stairs to the patio. The air was fresh, after the smoke of the gaming room, and the lights soft. And the show was on again. The girls, this time, wore long, much ruffled, white dresses (with no backs) and the men were in white, too—pleated white *guayaberas,* and white trousers and white shoes and white straw hats. They did an intricate samba—at least Pam, walking beside Bill Weigand, stopping with him on the bottom step to watch, thought it was a samba. It was very lively, certainly. It involved stamping. It was prettily gay under the spots; the dancers were in a pool of light with the tables and the people at them a low, dusky bank around the pool. From among the dancers, who parted to let her through, a dark girl danced—a girl incredibly slender yet softly shaped. She was not wearing a ruffled white dress; it was, at first glance, impossible to believe she was wearing anything at all, which would have been, Pam thought, perfectly appropriate. (It was not, on closer inspection, and by the narrowest of margins, true.)

"I wish Jerry hadn't come," Pam said. "Dorian—even Dorian—probably wishes you hadn't come." She looked at the slender, dancing girl again. "It isn't fair," Pam North said. The girl, dancing now before the others, with the others as a swaying background of white against her exquisite darkness, rippled. "My," Pam said. "Oh my oh my. Such a gay people. And so—direct."

She took Bill's arm and led him toward their table. She said, "You know, don't you? You get a certain way."

"I think so," Bill said, and held out a chair for her, and then a chair for Dorian. "It seems to add."

"A common denominator?" Pam said, and they looked at her. Very slowly, very carefully, Jerry poured scotch into their glasses; very carefully, he added ice and soda. "Between elephants and apples," Pam said.

"Oh," Bill said. "No. It's more deciding what to add—what is extraneous. You see—"

He was interrupted. Respected Captain J. R. Folsom approached and looked down at them. He had entirely regained his ruddiness and seemed in enviable spirits. "Lost my lady friend," he said. "Red-haired lady friend." He looked at Bill Weigand. "Thought you might like to know," he said.

"Did you?" Bill Weigand said. "Pull up a chair."

Folsom shook his head. He continued to stand.

"Went for broke, the lady did," he said. "Like they say."

"She tell you that?"

"Nope," Folsom said. "But—I heard. I don't say flat broke. Just bent down. Maybe not that. But she dropped a wad."

"And you," Bill said, "made a wad."

"Didn't see you there," Folsom said. "But have it your way. Baby's in shoes."

"And," Bill said, "shoe boxes?"

Folsom looked down at him. The gray eyes seemed now, as they had seemed before, by far the coolest thing about J. R. Folsom.

"Never out of shoe boxes," Folsom said, "if you want to beat around the bush."

"It seems," Bill said, "to be your bush. If you want to tell me something, tell it."

"Nothing to tell," Folsom said. "I told you there wasn't. Only, nobody minds having a little ready cash. What with this g.d. income tax. Sorry, ladies."

"That's quite all right, Mr. Folsom," Pam said. "One hears so many expressions." He looked at her sharply. She was very innocent.

"Like I was saying," Folsom said, giving Pam up for Bill Weigand. "If there was any little difficulty—not that there was—if there *seemed* to be any little difficulty, the galloping dominoes took care of it. The old s.o.b.—sorry, ladies." He looked suspiciously at Pam North, who said nothing. "The gentleman we were talking about, he's up the creek with his little scheme. See what I mean?"

"At any rate," Bill said, "I hear what you say, Mr. Folsom."

"Thought you would," Folsom said. "Not to change the subject, you see that little dark girl?"

"Yes."

"Wow!" Folsom said. "All I can say is, Wow. Wouldn't go in Worcester. All the same—"

"Right," Bill said, and then Mr. Folsom left them. He kept his hands carefully in his pockets, presumably to hold the money down.

"Meaning," Jerry said, "that he won enough to square his accounts?"

"Which don't need squaring," Bill said. "Yes, that seems to be the size of it."

"Except, of course," Dorian said, "that he could hardly have known Saturday night that he was going to win money today."

"Right," Bill said.

"And," Pam said, "elephants or apples—or good red herring?"

But Bill did not seem to hear her. The show had danced away, the lights had come up around the tables. Bill stood and looked around.

Captain Cunningham was alone at the table, where previously he had sat with the Furstenbergs. People were trickling to the dance floor, and the Furstenbergs were not among them. Barron was, again with the blond girl. But, as Bill watched, he led her to the edge of the floor, bowed to her, went off among the tables. Folsom was moving, with some resolution, toward the foyer—Bill thought it likely that he was taking his money home, and thought it was wise of him, although Havana is safer than many cities. Mrs. Macklin was not in sight, and when he discovered that, Bill Weigand frowned slightly. There were, of course, many places she could have gone—and one of them, of course, was back to the gaming room. If she had, it might account for the absence, also, of Hilda Macklin. On the other hand, they might both have gone back to the ship, although it was only—Bill looked at his watch on his wrist. "Only" was perhaps not the word to use. It was after one in the morning.

Captain Cunningham stood up and looked around. He saw Bill standing, and briefly raised his glass in salute. Then Cunningham walked toward the wide stairs. The Buckleys from Kansas stood at the top of the stairs and looked into the patio, and, even from the distance, there seemed to be a kind of delighted wonder in their young faces. Then, hand in hand, they walked toward the dance floor. The North American orchestra was back, swinging through "The St. Louis Blues." The dance floor filled and the night was young, dressed in gay colors for youth.

And, over the music, over the voices, someone screamed. The scream was wordless—high pitched, rising higher. It seemed to come from a distance and from the air.

In the instant, as the scream ended, everything stopped. The music stopped, and the voices stopped. It was, oddly, as if someone had switched off all the lights, although the lights burned. Then the scream came again.

People around the tables were standing, by then. On the dance floor, people were frozen for a moment, then broke from the postures of the dance and looked around and looked up. One man on the floor held his hand up to his forehead, as if to shield his eyes—as if he were trying to see something in the sun.

"There!" Jerry North said, and pointed, but by then Bill Weigand had seen, and had started to run among the tables toward the castle tower—the make-believe tower, which had seemed pleasantly ridiculous, and did not now—not now with two figures swaying, struggling on the narrow observation platform, against the platform's low rail—fifty feet above the flagstone pavement around the tower.

The scream came again. It was impossible to tell which of the two struggling at the top of the tower was the one to scream. It was impossible to identify the two. They swayed, grasping each other, in the soft green light which washed the tower. Their shadows elongated, struggled against the glass housing the platform circled.

Several were running toward the tower now—dark figures racing among the tables, then among the dimly, prettily colored palm trees. Someone knocked a chair over, and it clattered on the paving of the patio. And someone dropped a glass, and the sound was shattering.

Tenuous in the pale light, the two at the top of the tower seemed, from below, to be locked in a grotesque dance. There was a kind of unreality about their movements, as if theirs were the pantomimed struggle of ballet. But then one of them—it was impossible to tell which—screamed again, and the scream was real—hideously real. It seemed to shatter the night. It was a woman's scream.

Then, from somewhere in the area of the dance floor, a shaft of light leaped into the air and went questing over the top of the tower. It lost itself in air. It dropped to a point midway of the tower's column and climbed up—climbed slowly, as if climbing were an effort.

By then many had reached the paved area beneath the tower and stood there, staring up, reflected greenish light on their faces. A man shouted. "Watch out!" he shouted, meaninglessly. "Watch out!"

The shaft from the light climbed to the platform and held there, and held the figures in it. One was shorter than the other—the shorter was a woman, bent back against the low railing now, arched over it; hair hanging down. She screamed up at the sky, and now there was a strange note in the screaming, as if it came through water.

She clutched at her adversary—taller, slender, clad also in white. The light steadied, and the taller, the one who struggled silently, seemed to move like a woman too. But she was shadowed, as the light rose from beneath them, by the one she struggled with. And who held, who thrust away, that was concealed by their swaying bodies.

One of those who looked up from below—this one a woman—gave a shuddering cry—a long, shaking "Ahhhh!" of terror.

The woman pressed against the rail seemed to lean farther back, seemed to teeter on the rail. As if a signal had been given, those nearest the tower's base backed from it—backed into those behind them, so that the whole increasing crowd of those staring up swayed back, in a motion like a wave's.

But then the two swirled away from the rail, still in their strange dance. They swayed on the narrow platform which circled the light housing—the housing in which, it appeared, there was no light. It seemed now, from below, that the taller of the two tried to push free. They moved part way around the top of the tower, and, momentarily, the light lost them. . . .

Bill Weigand and Jerry North ran among trees. They ran on grass, then on the circle of flagged pavement around the tower. Jerry led, because he knew the way. But when they reached the door into the tower, Bill Weigand checked him, and Bill went first.

The lights which circled upward with the staircase were dim. They plunged into dimness and began to climb. The stairs were steep and narrow, and turned sharply in the cylinder of the tower. They clutched rails on either side and pulled themselves up. But their climbing seemed unbearably slow.

The heavy walls of this mimic Morro Castle shut out

sound, as they shut out all light save that provided by the dim bulbs. It was like climbing, laboriously, inside a dark pipe. And if one of the two struggling above fell—fell fifty feet to unrelenting flagstones—or if both fell, the climbing men would hear nothing of the falling.

They were gasping for breath when they reached the platform—climbed into the merciless white light—reached out for the swaying two, now again against the rail. Olivia Macklin's red hair streamed about her face, and she had her hands at Hilda Macklin's throat. The girl's white dress was torn from one shoulder, and on the shoulder and upper breast there were long welts of red, from one of which blood seeped.

Jerry had Hilda, pulled her back against him, and she did not resist, although her body trembled against his. Mrs. Macklin's struggles did not end so quickly; for a moment she writhed in Bill Weigand's hands, seemed not to know that he was not still the adversary with whom she struggled. But then, very suddenly, her body quieted. But she spoke, wildly—still almost in a scream.

"Tried to kill me!" she said, and momentarily swayed toward the younger woman. *"You tried to kill me!"* Hilda merely looked at her.

"She followed me," Mrs. Macklin said, and spoke somewhat less violently, but still violently enough, venomously enough. "To push me—off!" She pointed at the rail. "You murdering—" She had turned again on Hilda. She went on. She used a good many words in telling Hilda Macklin what she was. But Hilda merely listened. As she listened, she pulled her torn dress over her shoulder. She put a hand up and smoothed her disordered hair.

"I found out what she was," Mrs. Macklin said,

again twisting in Weigand's grasp so that she could look up at him. "So she tried to kill me—too. The way she—"

Hilda spoke, then.

"She's crazy," she said, and her voice was not raised. "No wonder they wanted to—she's crazy as they come. She's—"

It was all Weigand could do, then, to hold the struggling red-haired woman. She wrenched herself toward the girl, and for a moment almost pulled Bill with her. Then, whirling, she seemed to try to drag both of them to the low railing. But Bill had recovered his balance then, and held her.

"Be quiet," Bill said. "Do you hear me? Be quiet."

Unexpectedly, she obeyed. She became a heavy weight in Bill Weigand's supporting hands.

Then she began to say, over and over, in a kind of babble—"Not crazy, not crazy, not crazy."

"She meant me to follow her," Hilda said, and spoke evenly, her voice without inflection. "She—when I got up here, she was waiting. To push me off—to kill me. The way she tried before. We were fools not to have—" She stopped, then. She stopped abruptly.

"Yes," Bill said. "More than you bargained for, wasn't it? And I suppose it looked so easy."

Hilda looked at him. She looked at him steadily.

"I don't know what you're talking about," she said. "I don't know what the hell you're talking about, captain."

"—say I'm crazy," Mrs. Macklin said. "Can't say I'm crazy. My mind's as good as—" She stopped. She looked at Bill.

"You see how it is, don't you?" she said. "With everybody against me—my own children trying to prove—" She was shaking, now. And the worst thing, or almost the worst thing, was that her rigidly drawn face was unchanged—remained smoothly impervious to the anguish in her voice, the anguish which burned in her eyes. "Do you think I'm crazy?" she said, and now her voice had an odd, strange note of hope in it.

"No," Bill said. "No. But, now, it might be better if you were, you know."

She stared at him. Then her eyes went blank.

"She was the one," Mrs. Macklin said. "She tried to kill *me*. That's the way it was."

But Bill shook his head.

"No," Bill said. "You'd be no good to Mrs. Barron dead, would you? You realized that. That's how you knew she'd follow you up here. To see that you didn't—harm yourself. I suppose you hinted you—"

But he stopped. Mrs. Macklin was not listening. She was looking again at Hilda, who held her torn dress up to the shoulder nails had clawed.

"You won't get away with it," she said. "You. Or that husband of yours."

She turned to Weigand.

"You know who she is?" Mrs. Macklin said.

"Oh yes," Bill said. "We know she's Mrs. Barron. And what they were up to. And—that they weren't up to murder. Not tonight, or any time. Why did you use the sword, Mrs. Ferris?"

Winifred Ferris did not answer. She did not even seem to hear.

13

The sun sank behind the *Carib Queen,* and she sailed for Nassau. Cuba was no longer a dark outline on the water; as far as one could see, the western water sparkled empty in the sunlight. But they were not looking at the sea; they were sitting in the coolness of the smoke room, and three of them were looking, not without resentment, at the other. It had not, they told Bill Weigand, by expressions on their faces, and also in words, been fair. He had known something they did not know; he had deliberately kept from them what he knew.

Bill was tired, and looked it, but he did not seem perturbed. He said that, as for the last, he had felt entitled to some pleasure during what was, by intention, a pleasure cruise. As for what he knew that they did not—he had asked questions and been answered. At least one of these questions, he thought, stood out. After he knew, from Stein (who knew from the police in Cambridge, Massachusetts), he would have been glad to tell any of them who asked. None of them had asked. They had, he said, as much reason as he had to

216

see the question sticking out. The question was a simple one: Where was the motive for murder?

"Not," Bill said, "the motives for snooping in other people's staterooms. Not for trying to peddle jewelry, which was not yours, for your own profit. Not for, as Folsom admits, having a showdown with Marsh."

That, he said, was what he had stuck on, not realizing he was stuck on that. That Marsh was looking into a possible—but not admitted—shortage in Folsom's accounts was, certainly, inconvenient for Folsom. But Folsom did not appear to be a man to jump out of the slow simmer of embezzlement, even supposing it could be proved, into the hot fire of murder. And, one had to take into account the appearance of people.

As for Hilda Barron, who had posed as Hilda Macklin, and been paid to, and for her husband—admit they were crooks, mulcting an elderly woman and, toward the end, advancing to blackmail. But they were crooks, not thugs—they were not small-time robbers, losing their nerve at a crucial moment and losing it enough to kill.

"Admit?" Pam said. "Do *they?*"

They did not. Emphatically they did not. They were, ostensibly, shocked at the very suggestion, which Bill had made. But they were not indignant; if they were anything, they were amused—or as amused as a couple on the make is likely to be after the bottom has fallen out of a plan which seemed to be progressing far better than anyone could have hoped.

"Because how," Bill said, "could they hope that their victim would put herself on the spot by killing someone else? Someone they had never heard of?"

"I wish," Dorian said, "that you would start over. Mrs. Macklin—I mean Mrs. Ferris—killed Mr. Marsh because she was afraid he would manage to take her back—back to her son and daughter, and the house in Cambridge. She was afraid because she thought they were going to have her committed to a mental institution. You thought of that, and radioed Stein to find out, and he did and they were. You didn't tell us about it because you thought it would be fun and games not to. Or—because you didn't want to go out on a limb?"

"Well—" Bill Weigand said, and sipped from his glass.

"I," Jerry said, "opt for the limb. You were looking for a motive—I'll give you the weakness of the others—and you thought: Wouldn't it work out fine if Mrs. Macklin was Mrs. Ferris, scared out of her wits, assuming she wasn't out of them already, by the threat of the booby hatch. Terrified at the thought—"

"The poor thing," Pam said. "We're—we're all bright and gay about it and she—there was that blackness—that awful—And I thought she just drank too much." Pam looked at the others.

"She killed a man," Bill said. "Let's keep it simple as we can, Pam. She ran a sword into him. She tried, twice, to kill a woman—not a very likeable woman, I'll admit. But a woman who was young and alive, and wanted to stay alive. Let's keep it simple as we can. Incidentally, she says she didn't mean to kill Marsh—just to threaten him. She says the ship moved and she lost her balance."

"You believe her?"

Bill shrugged. He said it didn't matter a great deal, except perhaps to Mrs. Ferris herself. If she wanted the consolation—

"Is she insane?" Dorian asked, and immediately added that she knew it was a silly question, although pertinent.

Bill shrugged again. He said that that would have to

be decided by a jury—a British jury, presumably in Nassau. He was, himself, inclined to doubt that she was legally insane—or, indeed, anything more than a little "queer." Her motive, in either case, was not "insane"—or no more so than any motive which leads to the hideous disproportion of murder always is.

"To get back to the point," Dorian said. "If we conceivably can. Where did you get the idea? If not out of thin air?"

Bill managed to look surprised. He thought it was obvious. Pamela North sighed a stage sigh.

"Because," Bill said, "she went to such an unreasonable amount of trouble—if she was really Mrs. Ferris. She wasn't merely leaving a place which bored her. She was running. And, she expected to be pursued. Why else the trouble?"

He amplified. A person who merely "wants to get lost," on whom there is no other pressure, simply goes away some place else and stays there. He may change his name, but perhaps not even that. If found he has merely to say he likes it where he is and, if he is polite, listen politely to expostulations. But if he flees from a threat—to life, to liberty, or to sanity—

From the start, the most likely thing had been that Mrs. Macklin was Mrs. Ferris. But each effort to verify that supposition had been balked. The face-lifting and the dyed hair—those were obvious enough disguises. But they indicated a good deal of trouble, and not a little discomfort, had been gone to. But they were only the start. Mrs. Macklin was traveling with her daughter. Mrs. Ferris's only daughter was in Cambridge, Massachusetts. Mrs. Ferris had been in a hotel in Los Angeles when Mrs. Macklin was aboard the *Carib Queen*. And, Mrs. Ferris had been in California when Mrs. Macklin was staying at a New York hotel.

Granted a carefully, and troublesome, arranged plan, any of these discrepancies, or all of them, could be resolved. But one had to grant the plan—a carefully worked out change of identity. The working out was disproportionate to the occasion—if Mrs. Ferris was merely trying to avoid a loving family. The incentive for the masquerade needed to be more powerful. Mrs. Ferris had been described as eccentric. A euphemism for drunken? Or, for something more? Bill had wondered. He had been answered. The family had admitted they had considered steps to have Mrs. Ferris committed as mentally incompetent; they admitted she probably had got wind of it. So, when Mrs. Ferris found out that J. Orville Marsh was on the ship, presumably planning to take her back to a mental institution, she killed him.

"Wait," Pam said. "How did she know he was?"

"She knew her stateroom had been searched," Bill said. "Marsh had, I suppose, been looking for something to prove what he suspected. She knew that Marsh was a private detective who specialized in finding the missing. She put two and two together and got Mr. Folsom's little sword and went to ask. That was, of course, precisely what Marsh wanted. But he hadn't counted on the sword. She says, incidentally, that when a woman goes to a strange man's room at night she ought to have some protection and the sword was handy. She saw the rifle box was open.

"She is," Dorian said, "queer enough."

"Hilda?" Pam said. "How did she get into it—she and Barron?"

That—and about it Hilda talked freely enough—was quite simple. She had answered an advertisement. That had been, some months before, in Los Angeles, where the Barrons were somewhat on their uppers.

The advertisement was for a young woman who would act as a companion, and who would be willing to travel. The Barrons, who were briskly trying to turn something up, thought the advertisement worth answering.

Mrs. Ferris made the mistake of approving Hilda. Hilda took what seemed to be the heaven-sent opportunity of posing as the daughter of a woman of apparent wealth and—apparent credulity. "She doesn't admit that, naturally," Bill said. "She insists she was just sorry for 'the poor old thing, running away from those awful children of hers.' "

The idea had been to get what could be got of Mrs. Ferris's money, and, at the start, Bill thought—although he admitted he was guessing, on the basis of character—Hilda had been satisfied with fairly small peculations—ten dollars here and twenty there. (Which she denied.) She had given value received, or thereabouts. She had employed an elderly woman to pose as Mrs. Ferris in the Los Angeles hotel. She had mailed the letter from Los Angeles. (And neither of these things, as she pointed out, violated the law.) But then she found out that Mrs. Ferris had killed Marsh.

"How?" Jerry said.

"Mrs. Ferris says: 'They say I talk in my sleep, sometimes. It must have been that way.' Hilda says, 'I've no idea what you're talking about, captain.' Anyway, she found out. She told her husband."

"Who," Pam said, "had come along for the ride?"

"And to be handy," Bill said. "Yes, apparently. He says, 'Why shouldn't I, copper?' He's a little cruder than his wife. He says, 'Show me the law against it, copper.' I can't, of course."

The Barrons decided they were really on to something. They decided that what they were on to was

Mrs. Ferris's jewelry, to be handed over, but ostensibly sold in her behalf, in exchange for silence. Mrs. Ferris said that. ("The poor old thing," Hilda said, and said with confidence. "She really *ought* to be locked up.")

Confronted by this, Mrs. Ferris decided on the logical move—to kill Hilda. "Actually," Bill said, "she didn't know about Barron. Didn't know then there were two of them." She had tried to kill once, and pushed Dorian into what she thought was an empty pool. She'd forgotten the net, if she'd ever noticed it. She had tried again on the tower—had dropped some hints about suicide if pressed too far; had been careful to make sure that Hilda saw her go into the tower; had known that Hilda would have to follow her."

"Why?" Jerry said, and was looked at. Pam was gentle in explanation.

"Because," Pam said, "they couldn't sell Mrs. Ferris's jewelry if Mrs. Ferris was dead. If she was dead, it couldn't show up missing."

"They hadn't sold it?" Dorian said. "At one of the places on the street Pam followed her through?"

"No," Bill said. "Because Pam was following. Because they couldn't be sure how much she'd seen. Because honest people don't sell to fences, and they had to keep on seeming honest."

"Then," Pam said, "I did do something?"

"Right," Bill said, and seemed to have finished. He looked at his empty glass, at other empty glasses. He looked at the bar steward, who beamed and went off briskly.

"Cholly's slugging?" Pam said. "And my—being pushed around?"

"Barron," Bill said. "He denies it. I can't prove it.

As a matter of fact, I can't prove anything on either Barron—not with Mrs. Ferris the only witness against them. But, Barron. Trying to find Marsh's effects, and go through them. Find out whether there was anything in them that would tie the murder to Mrs. Ferris—and to make off with whatever there was. Because, of course, Mrs. Ferris was no good to them—they lost their hold—if we could pin the murder on her without their help."

There was a long pause. Drinks came. Pam broke it.

"Our first time official, or almost," Pam said. "And all we *really* did, that I can see, was to buy an alligator bag I didn't want and—*oh, for heaven's sake!*" They waited; Jerry waited with some trepidation. "I just realized," Pam said. "I left it at that night club. What with all the excitement, and everything, and not really being used to it. I always leave things I'm not used to."

There was a long pause.

"Of course," Pam said. "There'll probably be nicer things in Nassau. And cheaper, really. There's something about the duties." She looked at Jerry. "Isn't there?" she said.

Jerry started to speak, and ran a hand through his hair. He decided that he had, after all, nothing relevant to say.

A MR. & MRS. NORTH MYSTERY

THE CLASSIEST COUPLE EVER TO SOLVE A CRIME— MR. AND MRS. NORTH

Pam and Jerry North, a charming, witty and sophisticated pair who like nothing better than a very dry martini and a very difficult murder.

Enjoy all these Mr. and Mrs. North Mysteries

_____ **DEATH TAKES A BOW** 44337/$2.95

_____ **THE JUDGE IS REVERSED** 44338/$2.95

_____ **MURDER BY THE BOOK** 47333/$2.95

_____ **MURDER COMES FIRST** 44335/$2.95

_____ **MURDER IN A HURRY** 44336/$2.95

_____ **MURDER IS SERVED** 47328/$2.95

_____ **MURDER WITHIN MURDER** 44334/$2.95

POCKET BOOKS, Department NOR
1230 Avenue of the Americas, New York, N.Y. 10020

Please send me the books I have checked above. I am enclosing $_____ (please add 75¢ to cover postage and handling for each order. N.Y.S. and N.Y.C. residents please add appropriate sales tax). Send check or money order—no cash or C.O.D.'s please. Allow up to six weeks for delivery. For purchases over $10.00, you may use VISA: card number, expiration date and customer signature must be included.

NAME _____

ADDRESS _____

CITY _____ STATE/ZIP _____

705

☐ **Check here to receive your free Pocket Books order form.**